Published by Gothic U Publishing

Copyright © 2016

ISBN : 978-0-9860567-1-0

Book design by Doug Hicks

The 100 Nights

Duchess MacKinnon

This book is dedicated to two women who have been some serious roles in my life. Who have influenced and inspired me to be who I am today.

So firstly, this book is dedicated to my best friend Reva Bell. She inspires me because no matter how hard she gets knocked down by reoccurring acute pancreatitis and recently breast cancer, she always hopes she will get better. She never gives up no matter what is handed to her. She is not only the best mother, grandmother, and friend I know. She is one very fine person. This book would not have been possible if it had not been for her. She is the one who encouraged me to start reading vampire fiction again which lead me ultimately to create this world.

The second woman is my mother. As an author, sometimes our characters we create do have a base of reality. In the books Cassandra was raised by her grandmother. My maternal grandparents adopted me when I was three (and I assure you that is where the similarities do end). But forever, they will be Mom and Dad. To me I have always appreciated the great sacrifice they took to raise me. Some of my first memories were being rocked and sang to by her. The following memories were sitting in her lap as she read me books. I remember looking forward to the day I could read so I could read the stories myself. She encouraged me to write and to be creative. She never set limits on what I could do if I put my mind to it. She was supportive when I knew she didn't want to be supportive. She showed me that nothing is ever to late. After being a homemaker for years and years, she entered the workforce as a substitute teacher for Head Start. She went to college and took classes to get her credentials to be an assistant Head Start teacher and began working full-time. All after the age of 60 I might like to point out. She retired after she turned 80. If that can't inspire you I don't know what can. It certainly inspires me every day. Therefore, this book is also dedicated to my mom, Leona Hester.

Acknowledgments

I have had the great, great pleasure in working with a wonderful team of people to get this book published and they are the following:

Steven Hatfield

He was a wonderful editor and it was a tremendous honor to work with him. When he isn't editing, he is a software engineer. I am so profoundly grateful.

Jim

He consented to model for the cover several months a go and the vision I had for the cover is a reality. Outside the photo studio he is a valued friend and true gentleman.

Doug Hicks

He helped me design the cover by editing the photo and setting the layout. He is a fantastic photographer in his own right and a valued friend.

Angel DeFreitas

He lended his image to me again for some of the marketing material for the book. He is a phenomenal actor in real life.

Shelby Early

She gets kudos because she was the makeup artist behind the cover picture. She is a phenomenal hair and makeup artist.

Chapter One

The pain was unbearable and all she wanted to do was scream, but she didn't scream because she knew if she began she would not be able to stop until she lost her voice. She had learned that lesson already. In fact, she had learned a number of lessons very rapidly from the moment she woke up dazed and confused strapped down to a table.

The man who was looming over her was middle aged and very non-descript. If she walked past him on a street she didn't think she would have noticed him except for his priest robes. He was to exorcise the evil out of her he told her in a voice that sounded almost clinical. He didn't even have a noticeable accent. Repent her sins and she could go home. The problem was that she had no idea what sins she had committed.

"My father will kill you when he finds me," she said. Firm in the belief that her parents would make it right and retribution was just a little bit away. The man laughed. "Don't be stupid, girl."

"Stop saying that."

He told her that she was stupid quite a bit. He mocked her as she fought against her bonds. He then told her she was wasting energy that would be better served in that little thing called repenting. She did repent for whatever imaginary sins she had committed but he didn't believe her. One of the many lessons she learned was that she was extraordinary in her healing abilities. Her body betrayed her he told her. As long as she healed she would never be truly repented.

Finally, he asked her why she thought her father would come for her.

Well that was an easy question, was this man stupid? "I'm his daughter. He loves me."

The odious man laughed again. She saw a shape move but nothing prepared her to see her father step into the light. The feeling of betrayal was almost enough to bring her to tears. Nothing compared to the soul wrenching agony of realizing that the reason she was not rescued is because she was where she was intended to be. Yet at the same time she was instantly furious. He was supposed to protect and love her. He should not be the cause of her agony. He didn't speak to her. He simply turned his back and walked away.

There were hours when she was sure she was on the brink of madness from the agony. She didn't even understand why she had not died. At first she asked if she had died and if this was hell? Her captor just laughed. In fact, she believed he found her down right amusing as much as he laughed at her suffering. She didn't know when she started but she counted. Her body throbbed in pain even when he was not there. She was never comfortable. Just air blowing across her skin hurt. When he was cutting into her even her blood falling in streams down her body and puddling at her feet hurt. Lacking a bathroom, she had to do her business where she was chained which made her cringe.

So, she counted 1…2….3….4…. and she would stop at a thousand just to start over again with 1. It kept her calm and the paralyzing fear at bay though she did not know how much longer she could stand. Her body was healing slower. She stopped repenting because it did no good. She was starving and was in pain so much that she would throw up the meager amounts of food she was given. She was either going to die or he was going to give up. She felt like death was the most likely course.

The worst torture was that periodically he would hose her down with water. It was like lighting a match and setting her on fire. She had read about the Spanish Inquisition. She now understood why innocent people were willing to do anything and say anything just to end their suffering. The stake was probably viewed as a mercy if they hurt nearly as bad as she. Time stood still for her. She had no idea how long she was there. Was it days, weeks, or months? She had no idea.

Then it happened. She was half delirious that she wasn't sure at first. She heard the door shut behind him but not the familiar click of the lock. It was her one and only chance to escape. She had been working slowly on her bonds. Her blood made it easy to begin slipping out of them. Escape and live or stay and die. She was paralyzed for just a minute just in case she was wrong about not hearing the lock click.

She knew that if she attempted to escape and was caught she was guaranteed to die. She was sure of it. She took a deep breath before releasing her hands. At least she knew she would not die without fighting.

It seemed to take forever to get to the door because she was so weak she fell to the floor. She had to crawl until she could find something to grab hold of to help her stand up. She opened the heavy door and it felt like it weighed a ton. Hell, he didn't need a lock. Just weaken her to the point that she couldn't open it. But adrenaline was an amazing thing and she was able to wedge it open just enough to slip her body through. She collapsed on the other side just to look up to see a steep flight of stairs that lead to yet another damn door. Her heart sank at the thought that it could be locked. Especially as she could see the elusive light peeking from outside.

She had to crawl up and it was torturous. Worse she felt like time was going by quickly and that she was in danger of being caught. But at last she made it to the top and her hand reached out to turn the knob. She didn't realize she was holding her breath but when the knob turned she let it whoosh out and almost burst into tears. It took a tremendous amount of effort to push the door open as she was weak and it was heavy. However, she was greeted to a burst of sunlight that blinded her momentarily. She realized she was in a narrow alley. She saw out to the street ahead and it was bustling with activity. She stumbled towards the sidewalk which fronted dozens of shops. The first thing she noticed was that the landscape was all wrong. She didn't know where she was. She was brought back to earth when she started hearing screams and realized it was because of her. She was naked and God only knew what she looked like.

She looked down at herself and saw that she was a mess. Her unhealed wounds were oozing blood slowly and the rest of her was caked in dried blood. A man with grey eyes and long dark lanky hair grabbed her and she made the effort to fight back, "Shhh! I'm a doctor. Dear Gods what happened to you?"

"Must get away, he'll find me. Too close."

"He won't get to you. Jesus, you're just a child. How old are you?"

She felt a blanket being wrapped around her and heard paramedics arrive. She knew a crowd had gathered around her.

"I'm 12, I think? I d-don't know how long I've been c-captured." It felt like it had been an eternity to her. Perhaps it had only been a few days. It was later that she did the math and realized it had been one hundred nights.

"Shh... you're safe! I'll take you to a hospital and we'll figure this out." Exhausted she closed her eyes. She didn't open them again even though she heard the sirens of an ambulance. The paramedics and man were talking about her. Speculating what had happened. Her back was a complete mess and they discussed that she was going to have some significant scarring. She didn't care. She was free. She would worry about everything tomorrow.

Chapter Two

The following days began the interrogation on who she was and who they could call. She didn't know who to call. She definitely didn't know who to trust. She feared if they knew who she was they would call her real parents. While her father was utterly out of the question she was uncertain about her mother. She had no idea if she had a role in her abduction or not nor was she willing to risk it. She escaped once. She knew if she was taken again she would not escape alive a second time.

Exasperated the social workers and police finally said, "We need someone to call. Surely there is someone!" She shook her head refusing to speak. They guessed she could read and write. She was careless in that regards. However, every time they forced pen and paper in her hand she threw it and refused to cooperate. They pondered all sorts of wild scenarios. They sent psychologists in but for the entire world to know, she was Jane Doe. She felt that being Jane Doe might not be such a bad idea. Police officers swore to her that if she talked to them they would keep her safe. Safe from her legal guardians? She didn't think so. Her father was well known and he could buy the police if he wanted to.

She learned that she was very far from home. She was in Miami, Florida. She must have been put on the private plane and taken there when she was out.

Finally, the doctor that found her walked into the room. He had been treating her all along.

"Your back is fully healed now. Unfortunately, there are permanent scars. Care to explain how you healed so quickly?"

A few moments of silence. "You can pretend to be mute if you like. However, I am the one person you can't play. I know you can speak. I found you after all. I know something is up with you and I have a suspicion I know who you are. What I do know is that you are not completely normal, my dear. If I'm right about some of my suspicions, it will be most interesting. Also, you would be in grave danger since eventually someone will put two and two together."

"As if you can talk," she said with a sullen accusatory tone.

He looked started, "What do you mean?"

"Werewolf is the flavor I am detecting. I didn't know that shape shifters could be physicians. Isn't lycanthropy catching? It's labeled as a blood born disease if I am not mistaken. Kind of like HIV is."

"And what makes you so certain of that?" The doctor said suddenly defensive.

"I always know and I'll just bet you wish I didn't suddenly find my voice, now don't you?" She added spitefully as the doctor squirmed just a bit. "It's why this happened you know. I always know who and what is around me. It was just one of my grave sins. It is also why you have surrounded me with staff that has their own set of peculiarities. Would you like a list?"

"No, I don't believe that is necessary. So, who did this to you? I have a feeling you know."

"I don't believe it is safe for me to say who did anything to me. I have learned something in my captivity. You don't trust anyone and you keep your mouth shut."

"But you don't shift?"

"Of course I don't shift. I don't carry lycanthropy. Haven't you already run the blood test to check me for it?"

"Remarkable," he whispered. "Were you being tested for your healing properties like a lab rat?"

She laughed. "Nope, they were trying to exorcise the devil out of me."

"Never tell anyone about your healing abilities. Otherwise you might end up in a lab."

"I won't tell. Ever."

"Promise me," he commanded urgently.

"I promise."

"You're Alyssa Monroe, aren't you?" He whispered in my ear as he feigned adjusting my IV.

The girl kept her mouth shut weighing the risk. She knew something on the doctor that could ruin him if she told and she would tell the world if he betrayed her. "Yes. I am. My father gave me to him. I'll die if I go home."

"Is your entire family against you?"

She thought hard. In fact, that was all she had been doing since she escaped from her horrible prison. The only person she could think of was her great-grandmother. She never visited except twice. She remembered everyone whispering that until now nobody had ever even seen her. That she was a witch of some kind. It had been uncomfortable visits both times. She would look at her with a penetrating gaze and whisper periodically, "fascinating."

"Maybe my Grandmother? Well technically she is my great grandmother. My father dislikes her. I met her twice though."

"Do you have her number?"

"Yes, I don't know why but I felt compelled to memorize it."

"You might have had a feeling that you might be in trouble. Let me give her a call and see if you will be safe with her."

"Tell her that I am dead but I've been reborn as Cassandra James."

"Cassandra?"

"Yes, I need a new name and Cassandra is a family name. James was her maiden name. My f-father told me that once."

"I like it."

"I never did catch your name."

"I'm Dr. Norman Wolfe."

"How appropriate."

He flashed a smile. "I enjoy it."

"Dr. Wolfe?"

"Yes?"

"Could you arrange for some chocolate pudding?"

"I believe I could."

What Cassandra did not know or hear was when he left her room that detectives and social services were waiting anxiously. They too suspected that she might be Alyssa Monroe. "Well?" The lead detective demanded. "She would like some chocolate pudding," Dr. Wolfe announced.

"Did you get her name?"

"Yes. Her name is Cassandra James and I have the number to her grandmother. Apparently, she lives in Kentucky. She does seem to be having gaps of memory loss that I think will prove permanent. She does not know anything except her name and her grandmother. It would be unwise to push her. Given her injuries it is perhaps a good thing that she does not remember."

Chapter Three

Present day

I woke to darkness and fought blind panic that clawed at me. I tried to sit up but I couldn't and I struggled to catch my breath. I realized it was all dark because my eyes were squeezed as tight as I could shut them. When I opened my eyes, and focused I saw a pair of familiar blue eyes framed by dark eyelashes that some women would kill to have. I realized the reason I couldn't move was because he was laying on top of me pinning me down and I instantly attempted to try not to focus on that fact.

I sucked my breath in to voice a protest and he must have known what I was going to try to say. "I can explain lass."

"Mind if you get off me first?" I realized how awful that sounded and I winced the minute it came out of my mouth and I added quickly, "Don't you dare make a smart assed remark on it."

"I wouldn't dream of it," he paused and then added, "ok I would dream of it but I know better."

I had to purse my lips to keep from smiling. I was not trapped in darkness so I could smile.

Jared MacAllistar, the vampire king of Charlotte, NC got up gracefully like the predator that he was made into over 2000 years ago. Though I suspected his maker had more than enough raw talent to work with when he picked him. Sometimes I rather suspected that Jared considered me his prey. He certainly hunted me enough.

Vampires are real and he was the ultimate proof of it. He announced the existence of shape shifters as well and the world collectively laughed… at least for the first year or two. Then the reality set in and it exploded into one hell of a situation. A situation compounded by fear and the lack of any real knowledge of a new branch of crime that only existed in the realms of fiction. The world badly needed a Van Helsing. Instead it got me. It got so bad that some fiction writers were targeted by hate groups and accused to have known all along. Even now paranormal crime still has a long way to go. There simply aren't enough people who are trained to handle it. That is where I enter. I am the consultant for the Charlotte region preternatural unit and I am pioneering the first program in paranormal crime investigation.

Jared wisely had gotten a fair distance from me and was watching me warily. My lamplight cast shadows on his face that did nothing but enhance his features. Gods but he was handsome. There should be a crime against anyone being quite so compelling. As I suspected I was his prey, I equally was sure that part of me very much wanted to be. "You were having quite the nightmare lass. You were hurting yourself which is why I pinned you down. See the blood on the sheets and the red marks on your arms?"

I looked down at myself and confirmed that I had newly healed injuries on my arms.

"And you didn't enjoy it?"

"Well truthfully, with you thrashing about there for a while I did have a few moments of enjoyment."

"Lecherous piece of shit." I couldn't be too mad. On the other hand, perhaps I could. "Why the hell are you here in the first place?"

"You have not replied to my invitation."

I had to think for a moment on which invitation and realized it was the one on me coming to the opening of The Endless Night.

"Seriously? You are here in the middle of the night because I have not responded to an invitation? I suppose you didn't consider that I might not have replied because I don't want to go and was trying to figure out the polite way to say no without writing a hell no and mailing it back. Why do I feel like there is more to this?" The one thing I learned with Jared is that there is always more to the story if you want to probe him for it.

Jared sighed, "You're a hard woman lass."

"Quite so, now spill with the *real* reason you are here."

"I heard you investigated a rather bad crime scene earlier tonight. I wanted to check to make sure you're okay."

"You do realize I am not a novice at this? I did have to contend with Renaldo. Who told you about the crime scene by the way?"

"Nobody had to. It was all over the police scanner."

"And of course you have one."

"Of course and a paid staff to listen to them." I wondered if Detective Anderson knew that.

"You do realize how crazy that sounds?"

"Well given that the police have proven not to be very forthcoming in their information to me, I find that a little eavesdropping is not necessarily a bad thing. So is there anything you want to tell me, lass?" Of course, he would find out and want to know more. He was after all the leader of the entire preternatural community for the region and "rather bad scene" was a massive understatement.

Chapter Four

It was bloody and awful and in the most literal sense. Just when you looked at the scene you knew nothing human could do what was done or at least you hoped nothing entirely human could. The house was in a nice gated community in Matthews, a small yet affluent town to the southeast of Charlotte.

The first thing that I noticed about the scene was the smell. I could smell the decaying flesh almost as soon as I got out of the car and it grew stronger as I approached the house. With the metallic smell of blood pervading the air, my stomach clenched with the knowledge that I was going to be seeing things that I would have nightmares about later. Decaying flesh is one of those smells that you can never forget once you smell it. It's also one of those smells you hope you never smell again. The entire house pulsed with magick too. I wasn't going to get out of not going inside. Sometimes there would be crimes that the cops only hoped nothing human could do.

"It's an awful one, Cassandra." Detective Anderson warned me at the door.

"I can smell that it is. I have to go in unfortunately. The air is thick with magick."

I liked Detective Mike Anderson. He was a unique detective. Brilliant but lacking in significant social filters. It's what got him put on the paranormal team that some people were starting to call "The Monster Squad". The final straw was him whistling Jingle Bells over the body of a murdered teenage girl. He was too good to let go because he had the highest close rate of any detective in the country and yet he was a major liability to the department. He welcomed the solution only if they could pair him with me. He told me at my interview that he was bored with regular crime anyway.

He didn't look like your typical detective. He was sloppy. He looked like he tried to put himself together but not very successfully. He was a little pudgy around the middle, average height and build, and dark unruly hair. I put on the full amount of protective gear and went in. I wasn't sure which was worse. The gore or the sheer amount of magick in the air. They were both nearly overwhelming. I suddenly adopted a new mantra standing in the middle of it. I started chanting to myself, "I will not throw up." The bodies had been ripped to pieces and tossed any which way. The rage from it was just amazing. On one blood, splattered wall there was a message that appeared to be written in blood of the victims.

"Do not turn to mediums or necromancers; do not seek them out, and so make yourselves unclean by them: I am the Lord your God. - Leviticus 19:31"

The message had been on the wall for a while because it had dried to a rusty-brown color. One of the things I hate about crime shows is the fact that in scenes the blood appears red and fresh, even if the crime location is an old one. This was reality though and it sucked very badly. The one puzzling thing was it took a calm deliberation to write the message which didn't fit the scene.

As usual, Detective Anderson stood next to me as the scene was vacated so that it was uncompromised by someone's latent abilities.

"It's not an easy one, is it?"

"No," I said honestly. "There is a lot of magic here. It makes it difficult to pinpoint which one is which."

"Kind of like a room with a lot of traffic with hundreds of unrelated sources of fingerprints or DNA?"

"Exactly," I said, relieved, because he got it. The concept seemed to be a hard one for the cops in Chicago to grasp. Because I am very good at what I do, they would always assume that I was some sort of superwoman. When I failed to meet their expectations, I got a great deal of grief over it.

"Is there a way for you to work through it?"

"Oh yeah. I'm not excited about it though."

"Oh?"

"I have to spend a lot of time following leads. Also, if this is someone they knew, there is a chance I'll never know for sure."

"I hate to show this to you but there was a body that was left mostly intact. You need to see it." I felt suddenly apprehensive. He was very sober and serious which made me nervous.

He led me to a bedroom. The body was a woman with long dark brown hair tied face down on a divan sofa. On her back was what appeared to be a cross tattooed on her back, but I wasn't sure. Something had gone terribly wrong but the shape was clear. The similarity it had to my scars was very disturbing. I understood why Detective Anderson made a point in showing me. He was one of the few who knew that I had the design of a cross in the form of scars on my back.

"What happened to her?" I asked horrified.

"The M.E. says that she was tattooed and that she apparently was allergic to the ink."

"That can happen?"

"Evidently. She was in a great deal of pain before she died. Who did it to you? Your scars that is." Detective Anderson asked bluntly.

"What scars?" I asked defiantly conveying that I didn't want to talk about them.

"You're not playing that game," he said sharply and for just an instant I saw the real Detective Anderson. The one under the façade that I knew it had to be. He didn't have his solve rate by being a joke as some of his critics would label him.

I sighed and finally said, "Honestly I'm not sure. He was supposed to be a priest experienced in exorcism. He was non-magical though. He was your everyday average human being in term of gifts. He was only very evil and twisted. He was very ordinary. If not for his priest robes he could walk by you on the street and you would not notice him. After I escaped, the police tried to find him but to no avail. He just disappeared as if he never existed."

"So you think coincidence?"

"It might be." I said with not as much conviction as I should have.

"You don't sound very convinced, Cassandra."

"I didn't personally kill the bastard. That to me means he can come back. He was very thorough in torturing me as well. He hurt me just enough that left me feeling like I was dying but not enough to kill me. It was a very fine line he walked. I am sure I was not his first victim and if he is still alive I was not his last one. Let me touch the body and maybe I can pick something up?"

I was more disturbed than I cared to admit and the pieces of the puzzle just didn't add up. You had the scene of one crime that was brutal, violent, and filled with rage. Then you had this part that was calm, collected, and very controlled. It was like there were two perpetrators. One was calm and collected. The other filled with violent rage. If there were two, why would the calm one allow the other rage?

"I've been told that a tattoo like this would have taken several hours and then another few days for the infection to set in. The coldest part is that he also killed her by slitting her femoral artery so he got to watch her die slowly. What's even more disturbing is she knew that she was dying before his eyes and there was nothing she could do about it.

"That's cold, " Detective Anderson said shivering.

"Have the neighbors been interviewed?", I asked.

"Yes and nothing came up. The family was supposed to have gone on vacation. The only reason it was reported was that an officer who routinely runs and took the route by the house smelled something and called it in. We were called when they realized it might be a preternatural crime."

I reached out and touched the newly tattooed back with my gloved hand. So much magick was around that I couldn't tell anything definitive.

"She apparently fought against her bonds like nothing else because you can see how deep the marks went."

The markings were angry red with congealed blood but you could definitely get the idea of the image. If not for the infection, it would have been impressive. Almost what my back would look like if inked and not cut repeatedly with a knife. I wondered why he killed her. Making her live would have been much more satisfying since she would think about him every hour of every day. Every time she took her clothes off. When she would go into public knowing what had happened to her. Always questioning why, she was the sole survivor. I knew this because the man who did the things to my back was never far from me. He was my captor, my torturer, and he always lurked in the shadows just waiting to get me.

I bit my lower lip with frustration and I was angry. I don't know what it was but when I turned around to leave the room I smelled it. It was a very familiar sickeningly sweet smell.

"Do you smell that?"

"Smell what?"

"It's a sweet smell. It's nasty."

"My dear all I can smell is death and there isn't anything sweet about it."

"Hmmm," I said distractedly. "Maybe I'm getting a migraine. I smell things from time to time." Though in my mind it didn't seem like this was the case. Instinct was shouting that it wasn't the case.

"Are you done, Cassandra?"

"For the moment. Call me when you have suspects for me to meet."

Chapter Five

Jared was watching me intently. "It was a massacre," I finally said. "Half the crime scene was pure rage and it was done by a shape shifter. Yet just one victim was saved from it all and was tattooed before she was bled out. It was cold and methodical. The only thing that went wrong was her allergy to the ink. It reminded me of what h-happened to me. He tied her up so tight that she couldn't escape her bonds and she was quite the fighter. She fought to the bitter end. It took days. We believe the other victims were pulled apart first based on the decomposition so that he had plenty of time to linger."

"I would suggest that she liked tattoos and it was coincidence but days and the fighting of bonds, does speak of something else."

"Why don't you ask me what he tattooed?"

Jared looked at me with a bit of confusion. "Okay, what did he put on her body since it apparently is bothering you."

"A cross that is similar to mine."

Jared gave a very long, low whistle. "Well that was creative. As for coincidence…I wonder why the cross" Jared said quietly taking my hand.

"There was also a passage from a Bible painted in blood about necromancers and witches. The family just happened to be a home of active witches."

His hands were large like the rest of him and it engulfed mine, but it was alright. It was very comforting. "You're sure it couldn't be the handiwork of the man who did your back?"

I was startled that it occurred to him and hesitated before saying, "I don't think so."

Jared's eyebrows shot up. "You don't think so? Something makes you question it."

"It's probably nothing, but I caught a whiff of something that smelled familiar, but Detective Anderson didn't smell it. When the priest was torturing me, everything was kept remarkably surgical in cleanliness. Except when he was there…. he had a scent about him that was sickeningly sweet. It's probably nothing but I thought I smelled it. Perhaps it was from the decomposition."

"On the other hand, Cassandra, it might not be." He said quietly.

He was right and it was bothering me.

"I need to prepare for my next semester."

"So you'll be my guest of honor for the opening of The Endless Night?"

"I don't think so."

"Why? And don't give me the inappropriate line, since you know damn well it is an excuse."

I kept my mouth shut because he was right. As a premier expert it was appropriate for me to be a guest of honor. In fact, refusing would most likely be looked upon as an insult. I didn't want to do it though. I couldn't explain it. I felt compelled to be near him. To touch him. To have him touch me. I removed my hand from his grasp and I even felt slightly bereft. I started pacing back and forth without really intending to.

None of the books on etiquette cover situations like this. There should be one titled, "How Not to Let the Vampire King of Your City Seduce You!" or even better, "How Not to Seduce Your Vampire King."

"Sit down," I snapped as I paced back and forth annoyed with his height.

He arched an eyebrow and sat, clearly amused at the order. I imagine he hadn't been given a direct order in decades.

I said a little prayer that I would be able to stop myself as I stopped in front of him and leaned in and kissed him. Kissing Jared was not that simple of a thing. His mouth was warm and soft. I could tell that I had surprised him because I felt a hesitation but was a very brief one. Which was good. It would have been terribly demoralizing if I had kissed him and he rebuffed it.

Unfortunately, he was overly experienced with kissing and he was an alpha male. He drew me tightly against his body. His hands immediately entangled in my hair so that he could deepen the kiss. It was heaven and hell all wrapped up in one. Heaven because when I kissed Jared it felt right. Almost as if I was meant to kiss him and for those moments I was my most content. He somehow quieted the storm that constantly raged inside me. No that's not quite right. He just replaced the storm with one that was an entirely different one. It was hell because I knew I was going to have to end the kiss and try never to let him within arm's length ever again.

He rolled me onto my back pressing me into the bed with just his mouth. He broke off looking down at me with his stormy eyes. "Well this is a surprise," his said huskily.

"Why is it that you always seem to end up on top?"

He laughed and suddenly I was back on top. "I aim to please, lass. My motto is that a man should never quibble over top or bottom."

I couldn't help myself and I laughed. Then I stopped. His smile faded and for just an instant I saw what living two millennia really had cost him. It was an ocean of loneliness and sadness. I realized just then that no matter how full Jared's world really was it was with the knowledge that one day it would end and that he would perpetually lose those he loved. It was his curse and I felt like utter shit for what I was going to tell him.

I buried my face into his wide chest before saying sadly, "I can't, Jared."

His hands cupped my face and made me look back into his eyes. "Yes, you can Cassandra, my lass. You just won't. Until you can figure it out, I can wait." Then he added, "I have forever," he added bitterly.

I felt horrible and didn't know how to make it right.

"I accept your invitation as guest of honor," I blurted out.

"You dinna have to do that lass." I winced because when his accent grew more pronounced I knew he was more upset than he pretended.

"You're right. I don't. However, I want to and I should."

"Then you are welcome. I have to go. Unfortunately, there is business to attend. You're still coming for Christmas?" I nodded around the lump that was in my throat. When he closed the door, it was gentle but he could have slammed it and the click would not have been louder. When he left, I wiped a hot rebellious tear that spilled over onto my cheek.

Chapter Six

You would think buying a dress for the party of the century would be easy. It wasn't. It took nine shops to find the one. It was a moss green with all over black lace. It was strapless but came with a nice shawl that was black and moss green lace to hide my scars. The first shop, I thought the girl assisting would faint when she saw them. It was my cross to bear. My scars were a distinct turn off. Except for Jared who seemed to have no problem with them.

I picked up silver ballet flats to go with it all. I was smugly satisfied with it all. When my phone rang with Detective Anderson's ring back tone, I answered it happily.

"Hey."

"Can you come by? We have assembled the first group."

"Sure. Let me---" But I was cut off as my breath whooshed out of me and know I gave a little exclamation. It happened so suddenly that I couldn't tell if it was deliberate or accident. I collided with someone and I swear it felt like colliding with a brick wall. It sent my bags flying and I barely held onto my phone. When I was able to get my breath back the air around me was filled with an awful scent that was familiar. I looked up and for just a second I was back in the room that I was held captive in. Detective Anderson was shouting through the phone," Are you okay? Hello?" I latched onto his voice to fight the panic.

There was a note of panic in his tone and I couldn't blame him. After all it hadn't been that long since I nearly died. I had a scar from where I had been stabbed just to the left of my heart. I would have died if Jared had not personally made heroic attempts to save me.

"I think," I said as I gasped for breath. I took a look around to make sure of my surroundings "I'm near the Belk Center, Mike. I just got knocked down by accident," and then instinctively I faked a grimace and added, "I think I twisted my ankle." I figured it wouldn't hurt to hedge my bets. When I looked up I stared directly into icy blue eyes that I only saw in my darkest nightmares. My worst nightmare was before me in the flesh and all I wanted to do was run away. It was all I could do to keep myself from doing exactly that. He looked at me with a bit of confusion and it dawned on me that he might not recognize me.

I doubted my father told him of my existence. It was part of my arrangement that I made after not seeing to it that he went away for a very long time. He was never to acknowledge who I really was. Which suited him perfectly as it would be a major liability to his image. However, to be safe I made it clear that he would be charged for attempted murder if he did. It was a win/win situation between the two of us.

"Oh dear miss. I'm terribly sorry." He said in his nondescript accent and I struggled not to flinch or show recognition or fear.

He didn't sound very sorry but I didn't voice that opinion. He took my hand to help me back up to my feet and I fought the urge to yank my hand away from him. I then had to fight the urge to run away and say to hell with my bags. "No worries," and then I added, "I twisted my ankle though."

"Then let me help you. I can take you home if you wish."

"No, I was on the phone with my husband." Speaking into the phone I asked, "Mike are you still there?"

"Yes," he sounded concerned. In that instance, I truly loved Mike Anderson. He might be a bit of a nerd, eccentric, and the most controversial detective this city had ever had. But in a pinch, nothing phased him. I felt fortunate that he was the type that could take the ball and run with it no matter what the situation that is presented to him.

"Can you get me?"

S-sure. Are you in danger?"

"Oh boy you have no idea," with great feeling. "My ankle really hurts and I think I have to go to the hospital." I put as much urgency as I could.

"I'll be there in five minutes," he said in my earpiece.

"Thanks Mike, I am going inside an Irish Pub called RiRa's."

"Got it. They have a nice bench just inside the door.

"Let me help you miss," the man said smoothly and I had no choice but to allow him. So, I pretended to hobble being careful to keep my limp consistent and to put enough weight on him for him to believe I was truly injured. Once we got inside he got a good look at me and me of him. He had aged considerably since the last time I had seen him. "Do I know you?" He asked.

"I don't believe so."

"You're sure? You look very familiar."

"They say everyone has a double."

He laughed and said, "True. They do say that. Who they are though I have no idea. Sometimes they have been known to be wrong." He was going to elaborate and I didn't want him thinking more of me than I could help it. I cannot imagine what kind of havoc Detective Anderson had to raise to get to me so quickly. But he pulled up in front of the pub within minutes of getting off the phone with me.

"Oh Sandy, thank goodness I've found you."

"Mike!" I said putting as much warmth into my voice as I could.

He embraced me and whispered in my ear, "Play along," then he kissed me tenderly on the lips. I hoped Melina didn't find out or she might have a serious problem.

Detective Anderson turned and gave the man a look of sheer innocence. "Are you the one who helped my dear Sandy?" Seriously, Mike Anderson had missed his calling. He could have been a successful actor.

"I'm afraid I knocked her down as well. My deepest apologies."

"Accepted," he looked over at me. "I know you love the adventure of public transit but take the car."

He proceeded to pick me up as if I weighed nothing, which impressed me. Mike Anderson always looked a little bit like a mad scientist than a cop. He never impressed me as being very athletic as he did have a bit of a spare tire around his middle. So, the fact that he was picking me up like I weighed nothing was fascinating. Much to my mortification everyone clapped and I could see one waitress take the tip of a napkin to blot her eyes. And the Oscar goes to Detective Mike Anderson for such a convincing role as concerned husband.

The priest wanted to help but Anderson said, "No. No. You've done more than enough."

The man flushed because he heard the subtle insult and I wanted to groan.

"Well let me give you my card. If she has to go to the hospital, I insist on you forwarding the charges. I will see that they are paid."

Detective Anderson was going to refuse him but I answered. "Thank you!" I gave him the most wide-eyed grateful look that I could and took the card.

When we drove off, "Well Sandy, who was that?"

"My worst nightmare."

"And that would be?"

"The man who gave me my scars."

Detective Anderson was quiet for a few moments before finally saying, "Well isn't that a coincidence?"

"Yes," I was shaking visibly which frustrated me. Thank God he hadn't realized I was afraid of him."

"You're shaking Cassandra. Are you going to be alright?"

"I think I will be. It's just been a very long time. Smell the card. What do you smell?"

Detective Anderson took the card and inhaled under his nose.

"Some sort of incense and not very good quality either."

"That is what I smelled at the scene."

"If he was there do you think he collaborated with the monster who did this?

"I can't be sure. Based on what I know? I would say from personal experience no. However, who knows. He is fairly depraved. But in an anti-monster sort of way."

"Are you up to seeing some of our potential suspects still?"

"Yes. Take me to them. You know I always wondered what his name was. Now that I have it we can see if any of the suspects have a connection to him that we aren't aware of. Oh, and I want them all stripped to their underwear too."

"That last is unusual."

"Not really. It could be one of his victims. I can't possibly be the only one."

"No, you're right. You can't be. The connection is a stretch but we'll see."

Chapter Seven

There was a considerable amount of grumbling over my request just for the principle of the thing I suspect. Men could be surprisingly modest in the most unsuspected times. However, all the potential suspects gave in without requiring us to convince a judge to give a court order. Ultimately, I was told that when it was learned that it was my request, it cleared all resistance. Jared apparently had made it known in the preternatural community that complying with any requests I made would be rewarded.

So here I was peering through a window to see eight men lined up in their underwear. Everyone becoming unhappier by the second because the room was cold.

"I'll have to go in there. A wall is just too much. The officer at the door was not thrilled. He protested that it just wasn't done.

"Now it is." I said calmly.

He gave me a helpless look and Anderson said, "Just do it." The officer muttered under his breath but did as he was told.

When I walked in, I was met with a mix of anger, fear, and curiosity. The first two were not a good mix for shape shifters as it made them highly prone to shift if they were new and lacked control of themselves. I walked to the far end of the line and said, "Each one of you, I will have turn around. Also, I need to touch your hands for just a brief moment. I'm sorry but it is necessary."

The first one was quite large and it looked like he was very dedicated to his workout regime. His arms were heavily tattooed. "Hi," I said simply. He looked down at me and said, "MI 'lady."

"I'm going to need you to turn around me for and then I will need to hold your hands."

"That's it?"

"Yes."

"Well that's not too terribly hard. I think I might even enjoy holding your hands."

I smiled as he turned a full rotation. His hands were large but well-manicured.

"Can you really tell if I am a criminal by holding hands with me?"

"Yes. I can tell a lot about you by holding hands. For instance, you turn most appropriately into a bear. I can go on if you would like."

"That's not necessary. I pledged allegiance to Jared last year when I came to the city. Please if you could let him know that Rungsturn has been helpful."

"Rungsturn? Is that what you were named?" I asked curiously.

"Regrettably. I think my mother had to give me a horrible name because I kicked too much."

"I will let Jared know. You can go now. You are not the killer."

The second man was of a slighter build. He turned before without command and held his hands. When I took, them they trembled slightly in my grasp. "I won't bite you know."

"Your reputation precedes you."

"I know. You are all so willing and I was told it was because I made the request. Why?"

"I'm not sure if I am allowed to really tell you."

"Did he make it a direct order?"

"No."

"Then you can tell me."

"He will give anyone who complies with any requests you make of us for law enforcement a thousand dollars." I didn't know what to say. On one hand, I should be furious for the blatant interference but on the other hand it had made things so much easier. "I will tell him. You can go now.

"Thank you. Please inform Jared that I have complied with helping you. I'm Jonathan."

It went the same with the others. Each one being dismissed with our apologies and promising to let Jared know how helpful they were. When I got to the final one, when I raised my hand to touch him he flinched and said, "Don't touch me."

He was quiet and unassuming with plain brown hair and a face that was neither ugly nor beautiful. In fact, he was rather unexceptional and I was instantly on alert. The type that you would look past in a crowd because you wouldn't really see him.

"You must allow me. It is the only way I can conclusively rule you out."

"Says you," he muttered sullenly.

"Go ahead and turn around for me. I won't touch you."

He did but had to ask, "See anything you like?"

"Not particularly. Are you sure about me not touching you?"

"You don't have the right. I saw you doing it you know"

"Doing what?"

"Ogling them."

"You're accusing me of being inappropriate when I have a large police force observing?"

"Yes. You are like the whore of Babylon."

I took a deep calming breath to keep from exploding. I turned and despite the little voice that tells you not to provoke someone, I chose to put it aside because this was someone that needed to be examined.

"You're wrong on the fact that I have no right. I have every right to do whatever I deem necessary to fulfil this investigation. Rights that the Supreme Court of the United States has given me so that you would not be locked up but could in fact walk free. Touch is merely the most expedite thing to clear your good name but fortunately as we have your clothes I can figure it out by them."

"You bitch!" He snarled.

"Careful, careful," I said shaking my finger at him. "You wouldn't want to touch me. Especially in a rage. I'll be able to tell if you were a very…naughty…. little…. boy." I emphasized the last part to be as insulting as I could. "You wouldn't want that, now would you?"

I had put extra emphasis on the little part and I felt him loose complete control. I very quickly opened the door and slammed it behind me.

"Double bolt it! He is shifting."

The guard hesitated and I shouted, "Just do it! Or you're the first person a raging shape shifter is going to get to."

The guard quickly bolted the door and sounded the alarm that added extra protection.

When the first crash to the door occurred, the guard flinched. I pulled up a chair, took my throwing daggers out, and said "Now, aren't you glad you did what I said?"

The guard ran to the nearest trashcan and threw up violently.

Detective Anderson looked at me and cracked a smile and I rolled my eyes. "It appears you hit a nerve there, Sandy."

"Stop calling me that or I will be forced to start calling you Mikey and yes it does appear that I have hit a nerve or two."

He laughed for a good five minutes.

The guy's name was Sebastian Hooper and his rage lasted for some very impressive three hours. His determination to get through the door was amazing. Usually if an animal gets hurt from doing something, they eventually stop. It didn't help that Detective Anderson kept making snide remarks over the intercom that would goad him. I finally had to tell him to hush because he was making one of our marksmen laugh and we needed them on pointe in case Sebastian managed to break the door down.

By the time he was done he was bloodied and unconscious.

As they pulled him out I reached over and touched him gently and cursed just a bit.

"Nothing?" Detective Anderson asked.

"Nothing," I said softly. "However, that just proves something."

"Oh?"

"He's guilty of something and he didn't want me to find out about it. Look on the bright side of things?"

"Quit trying to channel me Cassandra. It doesn't become you." I ignored him.

"The bright side is that your locks are secure. If he couldn't break that door down nobody can. I know you can't hold him without valid charges, but you should hold him for as long as you can."

"Done. I will show the judge the video tape and get them to put an order to hold him. At least until a psych evaluation has been done on him. Go home Cassandra and get some rest. One of the officers picked your car up so it's out there. Try to enjoy the holidays."

"I will. I have Christmas dinner at the Endless Night."

"Really? Me too."

"Melina invited you?"

Detective Anderson blushed and I was vastly amused by it all.

Chapter Eight

I was looking forward to going home. It had been one hell of a day. I even smiled as I drove into my driveway. I didn't even mind the tedium of passing my own security system. My head was hurting from a tremendous migraine brewing. It was for that reason I blame not seeing it come. I had finished with the last check and heard the bolt unlock when I smelt the sickening sweet smell.

A hand shot out and opened the door and pushed me in, slamming the door behind us and locking it. I stumbled and fell hard though I was trying to get to one of my knives out of instinct.

"You know I thought I recognized you, Allyssa Monroe." The deep voice of my nightmares said in my ear.

Well shit.

"I always wanted to know what happened to you." He kicked me squarely in the side and I felt the breath whoosh out of me and I was sure a rib had just broken. Typical that he would be the type to kick someone when they were down.

"Likewise." I gasped as I fought back the pain breathing was having on me. "In fact," I added, "I thought of you every single day since I escaped."

"Fond memories?"

"No. I thought about how to find you and when I did how I was going to slowly kill you. You know I looked for you. I never stopped looking."

I had reached my knife so when he went to kick me again I was ready. I rolled pre-emptively and when his foot hit the ground I stabbed downward with all of my strength. I smiled when I felt it go through the leather of his shoe and when I heard a bone snap. Knife 1, Loafers 0. I almost laughed out loud when he screamed in agony. It was going to suck because it would mean that my blade was damaged. As he hopped around screaming, I got up as quickly as I could, even though it hurt like hell. He was still trying to pull the knife out when I managed to get my other weapons out. Apparently, my knife was stuck.

"Oh quit your howling. The neighbors will hear and you'll spoil all of my fun. I never expected that I needed a sound proof room. If you haven't guessed, I'm not a kid anymore and thanks to you, you've readjusted my way of thinking. I always carry weapons on me."

"You whore!"

"How tedious. You know you're the second person to call me that today. You would think that you could at least think up something original." I taunted.

"Devil's Spawn."

"I suppose that is the best you can do. Don't worry I don't blame you. The Catholic Church isn't really famous for encouraging originality. However, at least you could steer clear from the truth. I am the spawn of my father and since he gave me over to you, he must have been the devil."

He managed to finally pull the knife out and threw it to the ground. "I'm going to kill you with my bare hands!" He screeched as he lunged at me. I was ready for it and simply moved out of the way, making sure I stuck my leg out to trip him.

"What's wrong Father Morgan? If that is even your real name. Never had a victim best you?"

"I should have killed you when I had the chance." He grunted as he tried to get up from the fall. His foot was bleeding profusely from where my knife had struck him. It was going to be a mess to clean up later.

"But you didn't. Instead you had to torture me. You had to indulge in your weakness and play with me. You made a mistake and now you will die from it." I said grimly.

"You might kill me girl, but I will never leave you. I will always be there in the back of your mind."

"You're right. But I will have the satisfaction of knowing you will be gone from this world and that I was the one to end it. I will never have to look over my shoulder for you and you will never ever hurt another human being." I was ready to strike a death blow with my spear that I kept in a corner, just to have it firmly taken from me. I whirled around and came face to face with Jared.

"You willna kill this man, lass."

"Stay out of this Jared. This is my business."

"No. You think you will feel better but you won't."

"It's not your business and you sure the fuck aren't my conscience so don't even go there. I assure you, I will feel a huge relief when he is gone. Now give my fucking spear back!"

"Stubborn wench. If you willna listen to me then we will do it this way. He is under my direct protection, Cassandra James. While he is in my territory to harm him would be viewed as an act of war. I assure you that you do not want to test me."

Well shit. It meant that if necessary you had to fight the vampire king himself. To reverse the protection, I would literally have to kill Jared himself. I seriously contemplated it. "You unmitigated bastard." Of course, the man didn't believe in the protection that was just given to him judging by the snickers of disbelief. Also, the one loophole is that if he leaves Jared's territory I could follow him.

Jared turned to him. "Oh I think you might like the arrangement. If you stay in the territory, she can't kill you but if you do anything that displeases me I will kill you personally. If you leave, I rather suspect Cassandra will hunt you down."

"Damn straight I will."

"Of course," he said. "The way of your kind."

Jared shrugged, "At least I'm giving you a chance at a running start. Given that you just pulled Cassandra's knife out of your foot, you need it. You can start thanking me anytime."

I was angry and was ready to explode. Jared had completely overridden me. Worse it felt like a betrayal and it shouldn't have. When Father Morgan limped out because I had done some major damage to his foot, Jared bolted my door.

"Are you hurt?"

"Does it matter since I can't revenge myself if I am?"

"Don't be this way. Are you seriously hurt?"

"Broken ribs I suspect. I should be fine by tomorrow."

"I'll make sure he never hurts you again."

"That's not the point Jared. Oh, wait, since you pulled authority, my lord."

"Can I at least explain?"

"No you can't explain yourself! There is no explanation good enough for your interference. You know what he did to me! You've seen it! How could you?!? You had to pin me down because I was hurting myself in my sleep. You didn't ask what I dreamed about. It was him. I dreamed about him and the things he did to me! I dream about it almost every single night. I cannot even buy a simple fucking dress because of him because of my scars on my back!" I shouted and didn't realize that I was also crying until i felt a tear splash down.

"I know you dream about him at night," Jared said quietly. "I have heard your whimpers." I ken why you are angry. However, I think he is tied into those deaths, Cassandra and innocent shape shifters are being rounded up that were within a 10-mile radius of that place at random. Those are my people! I have an obligation to protect them!"

"All the more reason to kill him then? I have the right to finish him."

"If I am right he is linked to this somehow, he could not have possibly have worked alone. How did your father find him in the first place? He claims to be a priest. How do we know that he is one? Is he ordained by some Church like the Catholic Church? If he is a legitimate priest, then does the Catholic Church know about his activities? I'm head of this country's vampire council. If the Catholic Church knows about him and sanctions his activities, we have a very, very big problem, lass. There might be more than one of him. Why the design on your back? Based on what you told me of the other victim, why the design on them? It's starting to smack at being ritualized."

I hated it when he was making sense. I despised it and him.

"I hate you right now. You could have interrogated him. But instead you let him limp out of here."

"Oh he is watched. I want to see what he does in his fear and panic. I want to see if he goes home or somewhere else that will betray him. I promise you lass; I will personally destroy him once I know I have every bit of information he can get. And if you really want, I'll let you kill him. However, I won't sit back and let you do something without thinking long and hard about the consequences."

"Fine. You're right and I am holding you to the promise."

"Are you going to still be my guest of honor?"

"Yes, I made a promise to it." I said shortly and I heard him sigh.

"It shouldn't be about promises or obligations," he said sadly. "I would like to think that we are friends of some sort and you would be my guest of honor because this is a massive project for me."

"I found a dress but I think it's been lost in all of today's activities."

"I made an offer once to have a dress for the event. Just in case I had it made. Would you like to borrow it?"

"I would love to borrow it."

"I will have you try it on Christmas night if you are still coming over."

"I'm still coming. Jared, I do want to support the opening because you are my friend. How did you know to check on me?"

"Melina."

"She seems to share a lot. One would think she was a spy."

"One would think. She isn't though. In fact, I would rather she not share for her sake."

"What do you mean?"

"Just as I said. She needs to stop sharing. I don't think that if Anderson realizes how much she shares he would care for it. I'll have Jimmy pick you up Christmas morning at 8:00?"

"Morning? Dinner isn't until sometime after two, isn't it?

"We open gifts. You have a few under the tree."

I groaned as I was unsure of what to expect. I hadn't experienced a real Christmas since childhood. My grandmother wasn't really into it which suited me.

Chapter Nine

Christmas morning arrived with Jimmy calling me to let me know that he was on his way over. Jimmy and I met my first night in Charlotte. He was a freckled faced red headed young man that was Jared's personal driver. After doing some research I realized that he had a form of Asperger's and even though he was brilliant about everything to do with Jared's cars and maneuvering around Charlotte, he was simple when it came to everything else. Not simple because he was incapable of doing anything he wanted but because he viewed the world with a purity that I envied.

He always selected a SUV or common 4 door sedan to come and pick me up in. He was always conscience from day one of not wanting to cause as he said, "unnecessary attention." Today was no exception. He was driving a simple SUV with tinted windows. If it had not been the fire to my home earlier, I suspect my neighbors would not have known who I was. I was staying the night at The Endless Night in my own room. Something that I stressed. I rather suspect it was a room with a connecting door to Jared's suite. So, I had an overnight bag.

I shouldn't have been so easily convinced but I couldn't help it. Jared was very persuasive in explaining that it wouldn't be fair that Jimmy wasn't allowed to have a glass of the mulled wine because he had to take me home. After all this was his first year being legal drinking age.

I remembered what a big deal it was for me when I was able to have the freedom to have a glass of wine when I wanted to. I couldn't deny him his first truly grownup holiday no matter how I would rather not.

It was a very foggy morning so we were very close to the Endless Night before we approached it. The first thing I saw was one of the spires rising out of the mist. The entire place was breathtaking. It was truly unique. I was interested in seeing what it would look like once it was open. Jared kept the main portions of the Endless Night off limits to even me.

Jimmy talked about Petunia and her litter of kittens. Kittens that even though Petunia was frightened of the shape shifters and vampires, was utterly unafraid of them. In fact, Jimmy even managed to parcel off some of the kittens to the shape shifters as a result.

He chattered about the cars. He dropped me off at the door. I was privately disappointed not to see Jared standing there. "Where's Jared?"

"He's just inside. He didn't want to stand outside where someone could see him."

"Really? The GQ of vampires and he doesn't want to be seen out in public?"

"I suppose that's correct. What is a GQ? Is it another term for Vampire King?"

I forgot sometimes that Jimmy didn't really stay up to date with the latest news. "Something like that." I finally said.

"Oh. Well you will see for yourself."

Being given no choice, I opened the door to be greeted by a six foot four-inch-tall Santa Claus with fake beard. I took a breath to laugh and Jared said, "Not. One. Word."

"Couldn't you have hired one?"

"And break tradition? I swear they put the kids up to asking."

"They probably do! Do you have to wear it all day?"

"Fortunately no! Just when I do presents and you're late."

"I don't do well with the whole crack of dawn thing."

Jared flashed me a grin through his false white beard. He looked utterly ridiculous. It was all I could do to keep from laughing in his face. As it was my mouth kept betraying me and twitching.

"You're really finding this amusing, aren't you?"

"You have absolutely no idea."

"Come along. The sooner I get the gifts handed out, the sooner I can take this outfit off."

"Pity! I like the Viking Santa look. It could be all the rage."

"Detective Anderson is here incidentally. You're not the only one being made to get up at the crack of the dawn."

Chapter Ten

Jared built into his private area's structure a massive room. He called it a great hall. To me it was just an oversized room that was normally filled with wall mounted TV's, sofas, and chairs. It also had a table big enough for over 100 to sit. Today it was a Christmas wonderland with a giant Christmas tree that sparkled in the light with what seemed like hundreds of presents. A state of the art sound system pumped music throughout and there were a variety of children of all ages. The magic in the room almost shimmered in tune with the lights. Jared was instantly swarmed by the kids and I understood why he did it. To some extent all vampires liked to play human. Some were very good at it and some were very awkward. Jared was very good at it but more to the point he didn't just like it, he relished in it. His energy seemed to be fueled by his animal to call and his followers. He invested a tremendous amount into ensuring their well-being. In turn it made him one of the most powerful vampires in the world.

Somehow he had not managed to lose a critical part of his humanity despite the centuries. The constant love and loss, the immense power and command that comes naturally to master vampires can be corrupting and destructive. On the other hand, the one thing that scared me the most about Jared as he played Santa Clause is that he seemed to be just a little too calm in his skin. I knew there was a ruthless streak in him. I had seen it peek out weeks ago when he was fighting for his life. Maybe it was that he seemed to like being a vampire at the end of the day.

Detective Anderson was sitting with Melina but looking grimmer than he should have been and Melina was sitting stiffly with her head turned down. Now Jared did not deal with the gifts himself. As Santa, he had helpers and he sat in a huge ornate chair. Each child got to sit on his lap as a gift was handed.

One of his helpers seemed to be in a great deal of distress. She was beautiful with blue eyes and curly blonde hair. I moved and set next to Naomi who was looking concerned as well.

"Who is the unhappy blonde?"

"I figured you would notice her. She's having a terrible time with dealing with this. I fear she might shift if she isn't careful."

"Then why is he making her do this?"

"He isn't. In fact, he was not anymore happy about it than I was but she insisted and pushed it."

"What's going on?"

Naomi sighed and shook her head sadly. "Her name is Natasha. She's been with us from the beginning. She was born and raised in a small town in Western North Carolina. She got married at 18 and had a baby right away. A little girl actually. About six months after she had her baby she was attacked and turned into a were-leopard. Her husband, who was her High School Sweetheart, convinced her that she should go to a camp until she could learn to control herself and be safe for everyone around her. She agreed to it because she didn't want to hurt her baby."

"I've got a bad feeling that I know how this turns out."

"It took her a year to gain a good control over herself. When she was deemed safe for society her husband had divorced her and is now refusing visitation rights. She's not seen her baby since she left. We're at our wits end because the father comes from an influential family in the area and controls the courts."

"Is it ignorance or bigotry?"

"Both, I'm sure. So, it's difficult this time of year. She's shifted every holiday. Normally, Jared only needs 1 helper. However, as you can see we have six just in case she shifts without warning."

"That just sucks."

"The worst is her ex-husband has a restraining order that she is not to be within 100 miles of the child but he just moved here and is now trying to force the courts to make her move."

"So he is trying to make her leave her home? If she can control herself, I would testify for her and her control. Or talk to the attorney that is on the case."

"You don't have to do it, Cassandra."

"You're right. I don't have to do it. However, it is the right thing to do."

"I believe that Chicago is by far the poorer without you and I am happier for it because you are here," Naomi said quietly.

The gift giving process continued for quite some time. Natasha would periodically stop and hold a rather battered looking locket around her neck before continuing. Naomi kept nodding her approval. "It's amazing." She finally said. "I was sure she was going to shift an hour ago but she seems to be keeping it together."

"She keeps grabbing a locket around her neck."

"It contains a picture of her daughter and is one of her prized possessions."

"It looks like it has gone through hell though."

"It has. Jared's offered to replace it but she refuses. She's allowed him to make minor repairs and that is it. Even then she watches him like a hawk."

"Jared does it himself?"

"Absolutely. He once said he worked as a jeweler."

"Is it me or does it seem odd that he ever worked?" Naomi laughed a quick laugh. "He works even now but it is strange to think of him toiling as a laborer. He personally laid some of the bricks in this place though."

"Cassandra James." Jared's voice boomed. My head snapped up and Jared was sitting with a gift in his lap. I shook my head no emphatically; he shook his yes. The children oohed and giggled. When I reached, him I was as red as my hair. I flat out said, "You know I can't accept this."

"Aye lass. You can because you have to give it back. It's a loaner gift and I have you know it took me a long time to figure out how to make sure you got a gift and yet that you didn't have to really accept it because of your bloody insistence on partiality."

"A loaner gift?" I snorted, "That's a new concept."

"It took me weeks to think it up."

"Let's see."

"Hop up then."

"I am not sitting in your lap," I hissed.

"But lass, now is the safest time to sit in my lap. We're in public."

"Yes, in public. That is my point."

"Dare I hope you want to sit in my lap in private?" In a tone that was innocent sounding but we both knew was anything but.

I felt the blush creeping up and I was suddenly painfully aware that an audience was watching us and hanging on every single damn word, so I sat down. With the least graciousness that I could muster.

"Why do you have to be so incredibly difficult?" Jared murmured in my ear.

"Just shut up," I whispered as I ripped the paper off to find an unidentifiable wooden box. When I opened the box, I gasped. It was a Venetian mask with green and clear sparkling beads running in diagonal stripes.

"Do you like it?"

"It's beautiful. I assume it is going to match my dress?" I whispered.

"Yes. It will match the dress. I understand why you cannot accept it but I do wish you could keep it for real. I made it."

"You're an artist, Jared. Perhaps I could keep it?"

"Nay you won't accept it." He said with a smug air of confidence. "And why not?" I snapped.

"Those are real diamonds and emeralds, lass. It's probably worth half a million dollars."

"Real?" I asked as my mind tried to wrap around what real meant. When it clicked I almost dropped the bloody thing.

"I can't take this home with me for even a night!"

"I know. It will stay here until opening night. It will be delivered to you just before you leave to come here. When you leave from opening night it will be left behind. Will that satisfy you?"

I thought for a moment to find something wrong with it but I couldn't and truthfully, I didn't want to. It was beautiful. "Yes, that is acceptable. Thank you, Jared."

"You're quite welcome lass."

Bianca came in announcing dinner was ready and we all trooped over to the enormous table. Jared left to presumably change out of his Viking Santa gear.

Chapter Eleven

The Dining Hall appeared to have one large table but it was several sections that made it big enough when you got close to it. The chairs were actually benches which worked out. Each section had their own set up of turkey, gravy, mashed potatoes, stuffing, and vegetables. A fairly simple dinner which was good for the kitchen itself as they had to cook it.

I was sitting near the head so that I would be near Jared. Detective Anderson was sitting across from me and he was in what appeared to be a very dark brooding mood. "What's going on Anderson? You've lost your smile somewhere at the last crime scene?"

"It's this case. You're going to need to come in and observe. Just overnight, we witnessed several personality changes in Sebastian. When he woke up, he started out just as before though confused on why he was there. Very pleasant and congenial. Then he suddenly became angry and combatant and gave us a different name that was not so. Then another personality came and he was even more combatant and just pure violent. However, the one that disturbed me the most is the one that made it clear that he enjoyed inflicting pain on people. That was his thing.

"But nothing was a magical match to the crime scene."

"What if it was a different manifestation of his personality that you haven't seen?"

I sat stunned at the possibilities. It made sense but it didn't. The question that has been going on for years is the question of where does this magic come from. If he could shed magical profiles so easily could it be that anyone could do it or is it only unique to multiple personalities? Or could someone magical who kills be able to change his profile if he truly represents? The implications were dizzying and would change everything we know. I sighed because while I protested coming here, in truth I enjoyed aspects of it and had rather hopes to enjoy my bath.

"I'll go to the station after dinner."

"Well I wouldn't say you should do that. Enjoy today," Detective Anderson said with concern.

"No. If you are right then he cannot be released."

"If you're going, then I need to go with you," Jared said striding in. I heard a clatter of silverware and realized it was my fork hitting the plate. There were no other words for it when Jared entered a room. It took your breath away. His presence was always commanding to some extent but the man was just too hot. He was wearing a black leather kilt with a long sleeved white button up shirt that was half unbuttoned so you could see the expanse of his chest. "Where does he get them all?" I whispered under his breath. Melina heard me and said, "Rkilts in Stratford, Ontario is this one."

Detective Anderson blinked at Melina who blushed furiously. "As personal assistant I oversee his wardrobe. I've been doing it for years. T-that's one of my tasks. I don't just organize his schedule."

"Why didn't you tell me?" Detective Anderson asked stunned,

"I wanted to but it never goes well when I tell the men that I also dress Jared."

"Why not?" I would have laughed if he was not genuinely perplexed.

"Well. Just look at him. He is a good-looking man. Supremely so. Everyone assumed I would be assisting him with more than daily life."

Detective Anderson was truly unique in his lack of social bearing. It didn't occur to him that if Melina spent several hours a day with a man that was as handsome as Jared that he should be jealous. I finally intervened, "She was afraid you would be jealous and break up with her over it. Maybe even accuse her of being unfaithful which would hurt her feelings."

"Oh." The light dawned in his eyes. "You pursued me, Melina. Remember? I just figured there was something about me that you found appealing. Sometimes I wish you wouldn't share quite so much with Jared. However, that's something I'm sure we'll work out later."

"I'm trying to be better, Mike."

"I know. I understand that he saved you from an awful life. I don't understand all the details but I will. However, you will tell me everything in your own time. I'm a patient man. Besides I don't get pursued very often." He shrugged. "I think I should go in, though."

Melina looked startled and flashed me a pleading look. She had something planned and if I let Detective Anderson ruin it, she would be annoyed.

"Jared will be fine, Anderson. Besides I'd hate to ruin today for you and Melina."

"Besides," Jared said smoothly. "I have to drive because I won't be intoxicated. Then I can have Cassandra back here. She has a surprise or two that will be given in private.

I groaned and Jared grinned. "It's not from me. It's from others but you get so self-conscious when it comes to gifts it seems."

All in all, it was an enjoyable dinner. There was good natured bickering, laughter, jokes, pranks, and such. I overate massively and was sure that the new dress would need to be altered if I didn't stop.

Detective Anderson called ahead to warn them that I was coming and the vampire king would be accompanying me as everyone had one glass too many to drive, including him.

Chapter Twelve

When I arrived at the station there was a lot of winks and laughter. There were also some frowns and flat out surprise because Jared was accompanying me. When I went to the observation room of the isolated cell that Sebastian was housed in, I noticed the padding on the walls had been ripped to shreds. "Holy Deities. What happened to the padded walls?"

"I see you noticed they are no longer padded. Sebastian did it."

"How? A bear can cause damage but not like that."

"That is because he turned into a damn tiger."

"A what?!? He isn't a tiger. He is registered as a bear."

"Well ma'am, you sure the hell couldn't prove that to me. He turned into a tiger. Stripes and all."

I looked startled. It was always theoretically possible to be a pan-were. After all, if you could change into one animal, why not another? However, it had never been confirmed or seen for certain.

I went to the microphone for the room. "Hello?" I spoke into the microphone. He had been pacing but stopped suddenly and looked straight into the mirror. If I didn't know better, it was almost as if he could see through it. "Cassandra James?"

"Yes." I confirmed.

"Why am I here? I don't understand. I was told either you or a Detective Anderson could explain it all to me." He looked genuinely troubled and confused.

"You don't remember?"

"Remember what? I remember taking my clothes off and then nothing. I woke up in this room."

"You shifted multiple times, Sebastian."

"No I didn't. It's not possible for me to shift."

"Yes, it is. You're a registered shifter."

"I know all about that silly piece of legislature"

"We agree on that at least," I muttered. I didn't approve of lists that profiled an individual. I saw the good but I also saw the bad in it too. It was just yet another knee jerk piece of legislature that was wrong. The ACLU had a case that was sure to be heard before the Supreme Court though so it was likely to be overturned in the next year.

"I was cured of my disease, Ms. James."

"Cured?" I asked curiously. I could see Jared lifted an eyebrow at that too.

"Yes. Cured. The Demon that caused this, he was exorcised from me. I pledged my life to Jesus. I can even prove it."

He was so sincere and I realized that I had a true case of multiple personalities. Personalities that made sure he didn't know about them. Then to my horror he pulled his pants down and stepped out of them.

It was difficult to tell but his penis had something tattooed on it. I couldn't make out the design but it had to have hurt like hell.

Jared whispered, "Jesus." I looked startled at him. "That's what it says," he elaborated. For a second I thought it had been an expression of sympathy for the male genitals. Maybe it was that too.

"Cassandra?" Sebastian called out.

"Yes."

"Could you call Father Morgan for me? He can explain this misunderstanding."

I felt like I had been doused with a bucket of ice water. "I'm sure he could," I whispered breathing slowly.

"Perhaps, I should have let you kill him after all." Jared remarked casually.

"Well you didn't. It was the right thing to do because you were right." I said reluctantly.

"Ok. We'll call him. I am sure he can straighten things out. What's his number?"

Sebastian gave us the number without thinking. A police officer made the call and in a matter of minutes, Father Morgan agreed to come.

I took a deep breath. "Can you handle a pissed off shapeshifter?"

"Of course. You think he'll be able to get out?"

"Well he has managed to do quite a bit of damage."

"I can handle it, Cassandra. Particularly if he makes the mistake of going Tiger in my presence. I call all cats and once they are in form I don't have to let them shift back."

"We'll it's time to bring out the monsters. I don't have all night."

"You just want your bath." Jared referenced the luxurious accommodations of the bath tub.

"Well that too," I admitted grudgingly.

I turned the intercom on again and said, "You know calling Father Morgan isn't going to accomplish anything. He's on his way but it will be a useless trip. He is nothing more than another sicko. Like you. Do you think that we haven't pieced it all together?"

"Pieced what?"

The air changed, his tone of choice changed, and hell even his accent changed. Damned if Detective Anderson wasn't right. I had my killer. I would never have guessed if he hadn't had a temper tantrum. Nobody could have.

"You spent time there. You stalked your victims for weeks. You even almost loved them. You waited until they gave you the perfect opportunity. You didn't even have to wait long. Christmas is the perfect time. Families go on vacation to leave you plenty of time."

"You're wrong. I found them. Sitting like a plump Christmas goose."

"Ah. So, you admit it?"

"Bitch!"

"Oh. Wait. I see now. You were just a tool. You're not able to plan anything." I paused pretending to ponder on it. "You're the stupid one. More brawn than brains? A tool and nothing else."

He was screaming expletives and the air shimmered around him as he was almost mad enough to change form. I was about to succeed. Jared was looking at me with deep concern as I pushed the buttons. "You certainly have a knack of getting under someone's skin when you want to don't you."

"Shh," I said.

"So where are the brains since you're not it?" I asked.

"Come out, come out wherever you are?" I added in a singsong voice.

"Enough." He said and the magic ended like a running faucet of water had been turned off. A non-shape shifting personality had entered the room.

"That's impressive," Jared whispered.

"So you're the brains?"

"Yeah."

"How much do the others know of each other?"

"Not much. Sebastian was attacked when he was six. His family chose to isolate him by keeping him locked up in a room until the day they knew for sure that he would be a shape shifter. It didn't help that the uncle that looked after him the most was very fond of little boys. He was 9 when he shifted and immediately he was given to Father Morgan. Father Morgan looked for truly incurable cases because he didn't want to fix his victims. He wanted to use them as tools to further the church's agenda."

"And as a result you were born or did you exist since the attack?"

"I existed since the attack. The others were created as time went by and the need was necessary."

"How many are there?"

"That's for me to know and you to find out. Sebastian has not personally shifted in years. We shift for him so he does believe he is completely cured." He said simply.

"And when he finds out?"

He shrugged, "He'll be crushed."

"Does Father Morgan know?"

"I think he suspects but doesn't have any real proof. He also might know and just choose to turn a blind eye since after all, I am doing the Lord's work."

"So the last one killed the first members of the household and tortured the last one. Why?"

"But did I?"

"You're denying it?"

"Of course. I didn't do it?"

"You admitted to the slaughter."

"You know, Cassandra James. You're naïve. You will soon find that some things are much, much bigger than you."

"We'll see when it comes to this."

"Miss James?" An officer stuck his head around the door. "Father Morgan is here."

"You can bring him in."

"He didn't come alone. He has a lawyer and I'm not Catholic but a man who looks like he could be important is with him."

"Bring them all in and make sure you stay."

"Very good." He said.

I couldn't help but smile grimly as Father Morgan walked in, relying very heavily on a cane. He winced a little with each step.

"Well, hello Ms. James. Who knew I would be seeing you quite so soon again."

"Poor thing. Your foot seems to be paining you. Isn't that a recent development?"

"Yes quite recent and you know how it goes. Old age it seems."

"Getting old can be unhealthy. Fatal even," I added grimly. Jared retreated to a corner and was unusually quiet.

"So let me introduce you to a few of my friends. He pointed to the first man flanking his right. "This is Cardinal Butler. I'm sure the vampire king recognizes him to prove authenticity."

"Aye, I know him," Jared muttered darkly.

"Excellent!" He clasped his hands together pleased. "On my left is Patrick Fitzsimmons. He is an attorney at Fitzsimmons, Bowes, and Cox. They represent the church here in this area."

Cardinal Butler was fairly young looking for one. Late 50's to early 60's perhaps. He was tall and lean though not as tall as Jared. He held himself with an almost military authority. His hair was an iron gray and neatly cut. It was his nose that was most interesting. It was a veritable beak. It was hooked like it belonged on a hawk and I must have shown some amusement because he asked, "What seems to amuse you?" In a surprisingly cultured British accent.

So, I answered. "Your nose. If you had been introduced as Cardinal Big nose, I would not have been surprised."

I had to give him credit. He would have made a great poker player as he didn't even twitch. "It appears Jared that you have not taught this one any manners."

"Why should I? It's the truth. Even you must admit that it is quite the honker you have on your face. Even when you were just a boy it was quite prominent."

"Jared, you aren't police. Why are you here?"

"Cassandra needed someone to drive her. You know that I host Christmas and how it is very appropriate that the resident paranormal expert is invited to all major events in my domain. I serve copious amounts of alcohol for those who drink."

"Jimmy couldn't have done it?" I raised my eyebrows a bit at the familiarity between the two.

"Jimmy is 21 this year."

"How extraordinary. Has it been that long? I'm here to have Sebastian released. You are holding him without cause. Worse, you took him into custody improperly."

"What?"

"Exactly, Ms. James. Your Detective Anderson's police force was very naughty indeed. Sebastian is a ward of the church. He sought sanctuary when he was just nine years old and has rarely stepped outside the walls of the convents. I have power of attorney over him and I and all of my party have diplomatic immunity. Including Sebastian."

The attorney, Patrick Fitzsimons was a wiry man with geeky glasses. He pulled out of his brief case all of the documents proving the diplomatic immunity.

"Furthermore he said in a nasally tone, we are considering pressing charges against the officers that took him into custody."

"What?"

"Sebastian told the officers that he wasn't supposed to leave the church compound. He told them that he needed to consult with Father Morgan who was delayed on personal business." Cardinal Butler looked pointedly at Father Morgan's foot. "He asked them to call to seek permission. They told him that he had no choice and he had to go. Given his mental capacity he was compelled to leave."

"You have proof of this?"

"Yes. It's all on this CD."

"He confessed to murder."

"Diplomatic immunity tends to exclude but you have no proof. Do you have video of the confession?"

"Everything in that room is videoed."

"Show me the footage."

The police officer fled the room to get it. When he came back he was white as a sheet.

"It was turned off somehow," Jared said before he opened his mouth. The officer just shook his head helplessly.

"So no proof," Cardinal Butler asked?

"He changed into a tiger but he is registered as a bear. I saw the bear shape. He is a pan-were."

"They don't exist."

"Apparently, they do now. We have a witness to it and you can see for yourself the damage done to the padding on the walls."

"But it's not a crime?"

"I need to call Detective Anderson."

The phone rang several times before Anderson answered.

"You had better not be drunk because this is very bad."

"What's the matter?"

"Your officers apparently fucked up. They took Sebastian against his will. He was compelled. He was told he had no choice. Apparently, they claim to have the video of it all."

"Surely they wouldn't be that stupid?"

"Apparently, they are. Oh, and he has diplomatic immunity."

"The hell you say."

"I have a Cardinal Butler and Father Morgan here with one of the city's best attorneys.

"They are demanding his release?"

"Yep. Oh, and somehow the recording cameras in the padded room weren't recording. We haven't had a recording since he has been in custody and I had a full confession."

"Jesus, Cassandra. I'm so sorry."

"I don't care about sorry. Do we have to release him?"

Silence filled the phone. "Yes or no," I answered impatiently.

"Check the footage that they are claiming. I will call the District Attorney. I'm leaning towards the answer being yes we have to let him go. Do me a favor, if they really did coerce him would you get the names of the officers? I am going to want to speak to them about following procedure."

I looked up at the officer. "Detective Anderson will be speaking with the District Attorney. You might as well get used to the idea. We have to review their foot" He swallowed hard and nodded in acknowledgement and left. He knew what I knew. That we were unleashing a monster back into the world.

I looked back over at Father Morgan and smiled. "So how is your foot doing?" He looked warily over at the lawyer and then back at me. I moved in just a little closer and spoke low. "Pity you know. That you're not allergic to silver. You have no idea how put out I am that I have a knick in my blade that is going to be a pain to get out."

He took a step backwards and I followed. "So the lawyer doesn't know. But the cardinal. He knows about what happened? Just nod yes or no."

He jerked his head in assent. "Is Jesus over there in that room your personal handiwork?"

This time he jerked his head no. "But you know who did?"

A head jerked in assent confirmed a worst fear now that Jared planted the seed. "Doesn't it make you wonder?"

"Wonder what, Alyssa?"

"What you created when you hurt me." I stared him in the eyes and for the first time it was his turn to swallow in fear. "You're afraid. Good." I watched in the corner of my eye the Cardinal moving towards me but Jared stepped directly in front of him. "Stay out of it laddie," he said quietly. The lawyer was on the other side of the room rifling through his briefcase.

So I did the best thing I could think of. I raised my leg and stomped as hard as I could on his injured foot and was satisfied with his scream. He was howling in pain and Jared was pushing me backwards to protect me if need be. He scored a lot of points this afternoon.

He looked down at me with serious gray eyes. "Did you enjoy it?"

"Even more than stabbing my knife in his foot. He won't be able to run away if they lose control of Sebastian in there."

"We have a lot to talk about later."

"Yes. I do believe we do Jared." And I looked over at the cardinal pointedly.

Chapter Thirteen

It took another hour before Jared and I could get out of the station. Jared drove in silence through the streets and I was impressed. He seemed like he had a great deal that he was wanting to say. Things like I shouldn't have stomped on Father Morgan's foot. Wisely he knew better than to say too much because that was a battle he didn't want to take on.

As we pulled onto the Interstate heading towards The Endless Night he finally spoke. "I want to meet you and Anderson in private when we arrive. I think my suite would be the most secure."

"And the rest aren't?"

"I have a large number of people in my Endless Night right now due to the holidays. Humor me on this one."

"Fine. You know the cardinal?"

"Obviously."

"How?"

"It's a long story."

"It's your turn to humor me. I have time."

"I'll tell you the story when we are all together so that I don't have to repeat myself."

"You're in a bad mood."

"Yes, Cassandra. I am not in the best of moods so you might want to not try my patience too much more today. Oh, and we will talk about you stomping Father Morgan's foot in private. I was fairly certain that the Cardinal was on the verge of killing you."

"Fine." I grumbled more for principle than anything.

"When we arrived at The Endless Night, Detective Anderson was waiting. He was very grim and serious. He questioned why Jared's private suite as well but hushed after Jared shot him a quelling look. When we entered the suite, he did a low whistle. "It must be nice to have tons of money."

"Money is over rated," Jared said shortly.

"Says the rich," Anderson muttered lowly.

This was the first time I saw Jared's suite since everything was finished and I had to admit I was impressed. There was intricately carved oak paneling on the walls and crown molding surrounded the doors.

Jared had very good taste at least in what he liked.

"Jared knew the cardinal. How?"

Jared winced and said, "I should have known you would start out with that."

"It looked fairly important to me," I said casually.

"Cardinal Butler and I go back to when he was a boy. Periodically, I would leave the city for vacations of five or so years. My last visitation was in London. He was an orphaned pickpocket. I think he was eight or nine years old."

"What, he picked your pocket?" Detective Anderson asked grinning. Jared rolled his eyes. "Honestly, there are times when I don't know how either Melina or Cassandra bear you."

"He has good points, Jared." Melina interjected.

"So I've heard," Jared retorted his eyes twinkling. Melina blushed a deep crimson and Jared chuckled.

"Let's get back to the story," I finally said to keep us on track.

"Right. He was not attempting to pick my pocket. He was being beaten to a pulp by a man that caught him. I stopped the man which unfortunately took a permanent turn when he tried to do the same thing to me. The boy had been seriously injured. So much so that he was dying. Bleeding to death from the look of it. So, I gave him some of my own blood to heal him."

"Do you do that often?" I asked curiously. I couldn't help but wonder if it was a routine for Jared.

"No. Anytime I give my own blood it does weaken me for a time. You and he are the only ones in the last two centuries for non-changing purposes."

Curiosity filled me, "Do you make very many vampires?"

"No. In two thousand years, I have just over a hundred."

"Sometime you will have to tell me the picking process you use."

"Perhaps. My master made hundreds. Perhaps even thousands. Unfortunately, only a dozen or so of us have survived."

"Why?" I asked horrified.

"After six months, he routinely would force us to greet the sun. Sometimes sooner if we annoyed him and he didn't want to wait six months to see if we were worth his effort."

"That's terrible."

"It was a terrible time. However, every last one of us are not only Master Vampires but we have our own territory. We also all have done well in staying fairly grounded."

"What happened to him?"

"A few hundred years ago, one of his fledglings took major exception with his initiation and managed to kill him. Getting back to the cardinal. I took him to a convent that knew of our existence and he grew up and joined the church. I ran into him the first time when he was a priest. He was ambitious and rose quickly to power."

"So what do we have on our hands?" Anderson asked bluntly.

"I'm not sure. Whatever it is, the church is personally getting involved with this case. I'm not a huge fan of that. The Roman Catholic Church can make The Human Society and the Society for Humans Only look like rank amateurs. In fact, they were the ones who made us disappear. The real reason behind the Inquisition was to kill vampires and shape shifters."

When vampires came out of the coffin and it finally began dawning on people that it was not some sort of elaborate hoax, several hate organizations sprung up. My own father led The Society for Humans Only which I always thought silly. Almost like the little clubs growing up that kids would start like "No Boys Allowed Clubs."

"This could be more serious than you are willing to say, isn't it?" Detective Anderson spoke up.

"Yes." Jared said simply. "The Roman Catholic Church is of course the remnants of the Roman Empire. The church has a toe hold everywhere, knows how to keep secrets, and has unlimited resources."

"Well maybe it is nothing," Melina said brightly.

"Perhaps." Jared said simply. "I need to go down for a few hours. I'll be back among the living by midnight."

"I need to get going, Cassandra. Besides apparently, I have to have some very long chats with my officers on procedures."

"Couldn't it wait until tomorrow, Mike?" Melina asked.

"No. It can't. We just released our best suspect of the crime because of a technicality."

"I can go with you?" Melina asked Detective Anderson softly. "Of course. I just have to make a stop." He looked over to me, "You'll be okay with Jared?"

"I should be fine."

Jared and I were alone in the room in a matter of minutes.

"Our suites are connected via the bathroom, lass. I had locks installed on both doors if you feel it is necessary. With all that is going on, I would prefer that you not use them. I'll be back at midnight. We can talk some more then."

Chapter Fourteen

I opened the doors to my suite via the bathroom. I had not seen it since everything was completed. I knew I shouldn't accept any of it because it was highly irregular. However, the occasional visit couldn't hurt, right? I was lying to myself and making excuses but it's what I did when things made me uncomfortable.

Fortunately, my room was fairly simple. It was still luxurious but not nearly as over the top. My bed was a king-sized four-poster with intricate carving and there was a small room with a TV and a mini-bar area. Expensive but tasteful. There was a great deal of thought and care put into it. My bed was turned down and as I approached it I could smell the Lavender. A gift basket of bath products sat at the foot of the bed and I couldn't help but smile at it. It was a touch of thoughtfulness that I hadn't really expected. I sat down on the bed and found myself so tired that I kicked the covers over me.

She was screaming in pain. The room was filled with that sickening sweet smell and not her clean lavender sheet and the knife carving into her back felt like it was white hot. His voice was murmuring in her ear, "I've come back to finish the job. You will not escape me this time." In the background, she could hear someone calling her name. She realized it was Jared and she started shouting back. "Jared!"

"Cassandra?" The voice sounded closer. "Open yer eyes woman!" She realized her eyes were squeezed shut and opened them.

"Jared," I breathed as my heart raced. I was breathing hard and still a little disoriented.

"Maybe I should just go ahead and kill that whoreson."

I realized that I was shaking uncontrollably and I realized how lucky I was that I had not become something like Sebastian. Jared picked me up as if I weighed nothing. I was still trembling uncontrollably.

The bathroom was bright as he carried me through and into his own darkened room. He sat down pulling me back onto his lap and I didn't have the strength the resist. An all too common occurrence. I didn't have the energy to fool myself. I really liked him. He made up a large part of my thoughts. I liked everything about him from his hair to how I felt when he touched me.

Though the vampire King of Chicago did as well. He was a source of terror for me. A massive headache at times because it was always a game of cat and mouse with him. Charlotte was proving to be too much for me. I had a vampire king that wasn't trying to kill me. Instead he was trying to seduce me.

"You were screaming for me."

"He had me, Jared. He captured me and was torturing me all over again. To f-finish off the design on my back."

"Is it possible that this case is too much for you and you should ask to excuse yourself due to the personal nature?"

"No. I have to handle this, Jared."

"At the cost of your sanity?"

"Yes. Even at the cost of my sanity. I have to figure out how to stop this. He said this was bigger than me. There is something going on here."

"I heard him." Jared wiped a tear from my face and I realized I had been crying.

"What could it mean?"

Jared took a deep breath. "It could mean that the Catholic Church has resurrected the Milites De Spiritu."

"What is that?"

"A very secret order dedicated specifically to the eradication of vampires, shape-shifters, and anyone else that they deemed a threat magically. The church has very filthy hands. In the past, they liked to work with shape shifters. It's possible that this is what it is all about. They get shape shifters and they completely break them. The reason I know about it, is I had an assassination attempt on me. Fortunately, someone failed to do their homework and sent a leopard after me. My principle animal to call."

"I imagine that was disconcerting for the assassin to realize he couldn't kill you but instead you could order him about."

"Yes, it was. He was very unhappy with the realization. I hated having to kill him."

"Did they send more?"

"No. I made an example of the body of their shape shifter and they realized very quickly to step softly around me."

"Then why now?"

"I'm not sure. If they see me gone it would be a huge boost. However, I don't think it is that. I rather suspect that Sebastian got away from them by mistake. If I am right, it could be possible that they were attempting to break you to use you as a tool as well."

I shivered and Jared brought me closer to him.

"I will tear the world apart to find you if you disappear."

He was serious about it and that made me feel good. Jared meant what he said and that was important to me. Somewhere along the way I was learning to trust him in at least some things.

"How do I know you aren't using me somehow?"

"You have the option of saying no and I will not ask you for any favors for any reason."

"Natasha came up."

"I would never have mentioned Natasha to you. Nor would any of my people. In fact, they were under orders not to bring it up. You asked and Naomi saw a loophole in my specific orders. You would not have liked it either if you had asked a question and been shut out. They are under orders to tell you whatever you want to know."

I was stunned at the access.

"If I had not agreed to partner you for your opening who would you have had on your arm?"

"Nobody. I would have stood alone. Would you like to see the dress?"

"I guess," I sighed, dreading seeing it.

He took me down several halls. Nobody wanted to break into
The Endless Night. They would get lost. Finally, we arrived to the
room that had a door like a bank vault. He opened the door and
flipped the light on. The dress was hanging on a dress mannequin. It
was gorgeous. It was a pale light green nubby silk with intricate
silver embroidery.

"The embroidery is gorgeous."

"The thread is made from real silver. It will sparkle when the
lights hit it. The world will know that you have my protection. Not
even Father Morgan will ever dare to touch you."

I sucked my breath in because the statement could also ruin
my career. It could be construed that I was his mistress. "Bastard."

To his credit he looked confused. "You're awfully fond of
calling me that though I am not and I don't understand why I am one
now."

"Because you often are being one and that statement will
make it look like I am nothing more than your whore."

He closed his eyes, bowed his head, and raked his hands
through his hair. "You think too much, Cassandra," he said thickly
and slowly. He was very upset. "I am doing *nothing* that is not owed
to you. Even Renaldo made absolutely sure you were not bothered!"

I laughed at that one. "Renaldo did nothing for me in
Chicago! Except make my life as miserable as he could!"

"Oh lass, he did. He let you live, which confused everyone
that was prone to just kill you and be done with it. They couldn't
understand it. If you were unimportant to Renaldo, he would just kill
you because you were a nuisance to his business dealings. But you
lived, so nobody was ever absolutely sure what would happen. They
were 99 percent sure that he was not sleeping with you but you lived
and nobody wanted to bet on that 1 percent. If they killed you and
you were important, Renaldo would have had just cause to go to war
and expand his territories, which nobody wanted."

I knew I must have looked dumbstruck and what he was saying made perfect sense. Even more it would have been what he would do in his sick, twisted way.

"The speculation was worse after you killed Johann and Jeremiah. You weren't punished for it. Oh, he wanted to punish you very badly. He was even on the phone with me for the better part of an hour. Attempting to convince me to allow him to kill his regional paranormal expert."

I sighed and began to pace because I knew I was going to lose this one. I wanted to hit the damn man. Just the thought made me stumble. I was linking the vampire as a man and I knew I was screwed. I was screwed to start with but even more so. I threw my arms and said, "Fine! Dress me in any damn thing you want since what I want doesn't matter."

And I turned around and walked out with as much dignity as I could. I could hear Jared cursing under his breath so I picked up the hem of my dress and just ran blindly down the corridor. I knew he would be following me but I had to get away. I couldn't explain it. It was all overwhelming to me.

"Cassandra! Stop!" He bellowed which started me enough that I skidded to a stop He closed the distance between us.

"You drive me mad, Cassandra!"

I opened my mouth to retort and he pushed me back against the wall and kissed me and Gods help me, I kissed him back. He was fierce and passionate. He pulled back breathing hard and paced back and forth a few moments before he stopped. "I could seduce you and you would be willing, but, I won't. Make no mistake Cassandra. I want you badly. You are tearing me to pieces and nobody has ever done that. So I will not seduce you right now because I want all of you. I could not bear having you one night and never to have you ever again."

He stormed away and I slid down to the floor of the stone corridor shaking. It was hours later that I finally stopped. Peter, one of Jared's guards came to get me per Jared's orders so I could find my way. He wisely said nothing. Then again he never really said a lot. Even from the first time I met him when he was one of my bodyguards when dealing with the ancient vampire that came in town.

Chapter Fifteen

I did not see Jared again until the opening of the Endless Night. He would not answer my calls either. The damn dress arrived with a hair and makeup artist and I couldn't make my mind up on whether to put it on or not. Finally, I took a deep breath and muttered, "Serves him right if it doesn't fit."

"I beg your pardon?" The girl working on my hair asked.

"It's nothing."

I didn't think I needed someone to do my makeup but it turns out she was more than face. She managed to cover the scars on my back completely. I was totally impressed because I would never have guessed that it was possible. Finally, the evitable. It was time to put the dress on. It fit perfectly of course because Jared would somehow not manage to screw it up.

When I stepped into the mirror I literally didn't recognize myself. I looked like a fairy godmother had entered my place and I was Cinderella going to the ball. The ladies left, leaving me alone until Peter showed up. "I'm your bodyguard tonight, or at least until Jared takes over."

"I'm surprised he didn't just give me a reprieve."

He sighed.

"It is amusing that you are driving him up the wall, but could you just cut him a break tonight? This is a big deal for him. Don't spoil it with your, "This isn't proper," routine. If he kisses you, enjoy it. He won't go any further than that if you don't want to."

"Is he considering it?" I asked suspiciously.

Peter flashed a quick grin at me. "I'd be surprised if he didn't think about it." After a pause he said, "A lot. He is going to regret making the dress."

I sighed. "I'll consider it."

The routine was that I was going to arrive in a limo. I was apparently the best kept secret in Charlotte so there was a great deal of curiosity about who would be hostess to the event.

As we approached The Endless Night, it was fully lit up. The dragons that were carved were truly breathing fire. The gargoyles looked as if they would leap from their perches. Just outside there were fire eaters, jugglers, and acrobats. The first time I had ever seen The Endless Night it was impressive. You could see it in the distance and there was an energy about it.

"Impressive, isn't it?" Peter said.

"I think I know how Cinderella felt going to the ball."

"Well he isn't exactly Prince Charming."

I couldn't help smile. "No he isn't."

"I like you. We all do. Why can't you just accept that this thing with him is beyond even your comprehension? I am pretty sure Jared is confused as hell about it too. If I thought for one minute that he was the type of man who would go out of his way to hurt you, I would tell you to avoid him. If anything, you would hurt him because if you can make this work, if you allow for it to work, you will grow old and die. He will stay the same."

"But if I go down this path I might not be able to work as a consultant."

"Is it more important than your own happiness? You need to decide on that at some point."

"It's all I know how to do. This is who I am. There is nothing else for me."

He nodded in understanding. He opened a box and handed me the jewel encrusted mask. "This is yours for the night." I tied the silk strands around my head.

"So how is this going to go down?"

"He'll be waiting for you."

"Are you sure?"

"Yes. He won't make you walk in alone."

You could hear the squeals of delight outside the limo as we arrived. Finally, when we stopped, we heard yet another scream.

"Well that will be Jared making his first appearance. Hopefully there will be minimal fainting," Peter said dryly, "I'll get out first."

I could see the crowd and my stomach flip flopped and the most horrible thought occurred to me. What if I threw up from nerves in public? For the next few seconds my new mantra was this, "Thou shalt not throw up on the vampire king even if the bastard deserves it."

I hated being on display. Peter shielded me as he gave me his hand to help me out and I was profoundly grateful. "Be brave, Cassandra."

When he moved away, I was blinded by an explosion of flashes and I tried to plaster a smile on my face. How in the hell do Hollywood stars do this? I knew I was squinting but because I had no choice. I heard comments too, the one that I got was, "Oh my God, he chose Cassandra James."

I felt a tremendous amount of vindication with, "Is that even allowed?"

And more than a little insulted by, "But she isn't really all that pretty!"

When the flashes died down I saw Jared standing halfway down the red carpet. He was gorgeous. He was wearing yet another leather kilt but without a sporran. His shirt was one laced up the front with the top open exposing part of his chest. His hair was smoothed back and tied in a ponytail. In one ear he even added a diamond stud. For the first time, I was glad I had worn the damn dress. My mouth went dry and I was just a little breathless. He began to bow with a flourish and I suppose I got caught up in the moment because I found myself curtseying. Those damn etiquette classes that Renaldo forced me to attend or he would kill a cop were worth it. My curtsey was a huge mistake as the crowd and more to the point the photographers went wild and I was blinded again. When I could see again, Jared outstretched his hand and I walked towards him. I placed my hand on his arm and he escorted me down the red carpet and into the Endless Night.

"Gods, you're beautiful tonight, Cassandra. I think my mouth went dry."

"Well not according to one."

"Jealousy. When we enter, we'll head straight to the center of the room. Just follow my lead. We'll dance and that is it."

"What? I can't dance!"

"Again, just follow my lead."

"No, you don't understand, I am horrible. I couldn't find the beat of a song if my life depended upon it. I have two left feet and you said nothing about dancing."

"It must have slipped my mind."

"The hell you say."

"Let's go." He started moving and I had no choice but to go with him.

"Smile," he instructed as the crowds cheered.

So I smiled but added, "I was a bit preoccupied on how to avoid tripping on my own two feet in public."

Jared laughed and the crowd sighed. "It'll be a learning experience, lass. You are about to find out how powerful I can in fact be. It's something you have never seen before."

"It better be good."

"It will be if it works."

The roof was curved into a huge crystal dome and beneath it was a sectioned off space. Jared maneuvered us into the center and music began to play. He really was excellent at leading. I had no choice but to keep up but somehow I felt graceful in playing catch up. "You're doing excellent," he murmured in my ear.

"You'll pay for this."

"Don't make promises you can't keep. Are you ready?"

"For what?"

He stepped up into thin air and so did I.

"It feels solid underneath me."

"Well don't stomp your foot, please. This is not that easy."

We turned and he stepped up again with me following. At first the crowd didn't realize what was happening but the higher we rose the more they realized what was going on.

We were very high up when he stepped up again and I had to say something. "Show off."

"I've made a decision about you lass."

"Should I be worried?"

"I'll let you decide for yourself on it. I am going to court you and I will eventually seduce you. This thing between us isn't going to go away."

"I wish you wouldn't," I said softly as my heart raced.

"I know. I've tried to leave you alone. To be as hands off as I could be and it just isn't working. If you were honest with yourself, you would agree."

I was quiet for a few minutes before finally saying, "Yes, I know."

"At least you know that much."

"Just so that you are aware that I have every intention of fighting it."

"It wouldn't be you if you didn't."

The music came to a climax, fireworks began to fire above the crystal dome causing thousands of rainbows to shimmer, and Jared kissed me softly. It was a different type of kiss because it was more of a promise than the passionate explosion that was typical between him and I. With the lights and show below nobody saw what happened.

Chapter Sixteen

The rest of the night flew by without incident. The day after, I did not hear from Jared and it was not until the next day that anything came up. Detective Anderson called me, "Cassandra, I think you should come down to the office."

"Why?"

"I have something to show you."

"And?"

"Seeing is believing."

"I don't quite understand."

"Just come here. This is very, very serious."

When I arrived, everyone kept turning their heads trying to hide smiles and smirks. I finally got hit with an overwhelming powerful smell of flowers.

When I stepped into room there were hundreds of roses and all I could say was, "Oh. My. God. I'm going to kill him."

"I told you seeing was believing," Detective Anderson said cheerfully.

"I'm going to kill him. I am going to take my sword, go to The Endless Night, and chop his head off for doing this." And I meant it.

"What does Jared have to do with it?"

"Didn't he send the flowers?"

"Of course not. Look at the cards on the arrangements. Apparently, you have fans now. I understand there is even a Facebook page dedicated just to you."

"But why?

"In case you didn't notice you were exceptionally attractive at the opening of The Endless Night. There were a lot of people there with cameras. Men and even a few women noticed and are now showing you their appreciation."

"This is a disaster."

"Now why did you automatically think it was Jared?"

I could feel me flushing. "He said he is going to court and seduce me."

"Ah."

"What do you mean?"

"I wondered when he was going to decide to make the move."

"What? You knew and didn't tell me?"

"No offense Cassandra but you have been playing hard to get with him."

"I have not been playing. I just…"

"Don't you dare tell me you are not interested, because we both know that is a lie. For all him being a vampire he is still a man and you are very aware of that."

"If I were to allow myself, I would have to give this up. And consulting has been my whole life. I was trained specifically for this job. I honestly don't know what I would do with myself."

"Is that all Cassandra? I don't buy that excuse. As long as I am head of this division, and believe me, I am not going anywhere because nobody wants this bloody job, you will consult for me. In fact, if I cannot have you, I will step down."

"You're being very perceptive this morning," I grumbled.

"I know. The fact that I can spell it out should be a big bright shiny neon sign for you on what everyone is seeing."

"I don't trust him, Mike. I want to, but, what if at the end of the day I cannot and he gives up on me?"

"Then he is not worthy of you, but, you will never know until you try to open yourself up. Do I trust him? To some extent yes. I understand him a bit better through Melina and I understand that he is fiercely protective of those he cares about. Plus, I doubt very seriously that he would give up. Now look at this, Cassandra James. This is me, the social klutz giving you advice."

"You're not all that bad."

"Tell that to the family of the victim that objected to me whistling Jingle Bells over their dead daughter's corpse."

"So you think I should just let him do his thing?"

"Yes. So now for our little problem."

"What little problem?"

Detective Anderson sighed. "The flowers. This is a police station, not a florist."

Chapter Seventeen

Everything was quiet for just a little over a week. The flowers finally stopped which was good because we were running out of places to send them. By the end of it, we had a tremendous amount of goodwill from the dying, sick, elderly, and cemeteries because we sent the flowers to nursing homes, hospices, hospitals, and graveyards.

I had not heard one word from Jared but I knew he was planning something. By all accounts the Endless Night was a huge hit and reproductions of the dress I wore were flooding the market because nobody knew who the designer was and Jared was keeping quiet about it.

But I knew he was there. The crime scene was going cold much to my frustration. On top of it all, the semester was about to begin so that my time would be divided between the two things. I had to deal with Natasha's case which I dreaded with great trepidation since I wasn't well loved because I refused to have charges stick to my father.

The attorney representing her husband was Emanuel Pennington. He was oily. That was the best way to describe him. It wasn't just his hair or his rat-like nose. It was just his entire demeanor. I didn't like him very much. You could almost suggest hate on first sight. The worst part of him was he had a whiney, nasally voice which just grated on your nerves. If he had been the owner of a used car dealership, you would say he fit in just fine. I imagine he won a lot of cases if for no other reason so that you could shut him up.

"Ms. James, my secretary said you were most insistent on seeing me. Usually I don't grant audiences without an appointment."

"I realize that, but you are working on a case against Natasha Robinson."

"Ah the dangerous shapeshifter."

"She isn't and I think you know that."

"I don't know what you can be talking about? Even she has admitted she is a danger."

"When?"

"Several years ago when she gave custody."

"She was correct and did the most responsible thing."

"Abandoning her child was responsible?"

"Yes. In her case, it was, but as you are well aware your client agreed for it to be a temporary arrangement after being talked into it by your client. He was after all married to her and it was a reasonable assumption that she would not have him try to strip her parental rights."

"It's best for the child. He has moved on and remarried. The child does not even remember her mother."

I shook my head. "You're going to try to prove that she isn't safe?"

"Of course."

"Good luck. I am being subpoenaed to testify for her. I witnessed her remarkable control." I smiled in satisfaction when his face went a few shades of white.

"Don't be hasty."

"No," I said very simply. "You don't be hasty. I'm sure she is willing to deal fairly with you if you would give her a chance. But you have her labeled as nothing more than a monster and not deserving of the time of day. You are wanting to remove her from a safe home where she has gainful employment, a good roof over her head, and friends. I am sure you have heard that The Endless Night has had a wonderful success? Apparently, my appearance inspired a fan page in my honor. Should I make a comment on the fan page about how unfairly shapeshifters are being dealt with?

If you attempt to make her move you are going to be presented with a case of a poor young woman who tragically became the victim of a cruel shape shifter. She sought the help she needed at the insistence of the love of her life so that she could have control and be a good mother. She comes back just to be victimized a second time by her husband who divorced her and now prevents her from seeing her only child. Furthermore, we now see her in a position where she has community, a job, and a place to live outside of the restraining order zone and you are trying to victimize her a third time by forcing her to leave everything based on his decisions.

I read the case notes too about what happened to her. I am asking questions about the circumstances of that encounter."

The lawyer was white. I had thrown the last as a shot in the dark so that meant I was onto something. I would remember to tell Jared about it. "What kind of terms does she want?"

"She doesn't have to move; your client will cease to stop that. She gets visitation every other weekend. No exceptions or games. Visitations will be supervised of course by our own community members. She will never be left alone at The Endless Night. And alternating Christmas and Thanksgivings. The first three years every Christmas. That's fair I think."

"Not unusual, no," He said frowning. "Are you done with me, Ms. James? I have a client to talk into these terms."

"How are you going to pitch it to him?"

"That his ex-wife and mother of the child has someone that can testify about her level of control and that you're impossible to discredit right now. That he has a choice of losing complete custody at the whim of the vampire king who has hired the best family law attorney in the state or to make the concessions. That if he is smart he will not push things or he might be on the receiving end of losing his parental rights. I am sure he has hired the best or you would not be speaking to me? Also, there are new questions about that happened to the mother of the child and that if he agrees those questions will go away"

"Absolutely the very best that money can buy and yes I could restrain myself."

"Dare I hope to never lay eyes on you again?"

"Then I advise not getting involved in family law matters that involve shapeshifters."

I turned and walked out.

Chapter Eighteen

Life is filled with mundane tasks. Mine is no exception. I have to eat and wash dishes like anyone else. My doorbell rang and I stopped what I was doing. I had been taught well enough not to just open my door to anyone, so I glanced at the video monitor and sighed.

Jared was standing there waiting to be let in.

"You're talking to me again?" I asked when I opened the door.

"I never stopped talking to you, lass."

"It's been weeks."

"Did you miss me?"

"Of course not!" I lied and Jared smiled with the self-confidence of a man who knew. He infuriated me with his arrogance and confidence.

"I told you lass. I was going to court and seduce you. How can I do that by not talking to you?" I flushed at that. "I would rather you did neither"

"Would you honestly be happier if I didn't try?"

He had me there. I didn't know. If he had never kissed me, the answer would be a resounding yes. But he did kiss me and I did return it with a great deal of enthusiasm. I swallowed around the lump in my throat and answered the best I could, "I don't know."

"At least you're being honest with yourself."

"Peter says that I should give you a break."

"Your resistance to me, does it have anything to do with how you got your scars?"

I blushed again. "No."

"Then do you mind clueing me in? I have the feeling that there is much more to this."

"Not yet."

Jared swore an oath and began pacing. His energy was nearly overwhelming. I closed my eyes to find my center. He stopped moving and when I opened my eyes I was looking directly into blue intense ones.

"I'm going to kiss you, Cassandra." I licked my lips out of reflex and somehow found my voice, though it was a whisper.

"I know, Jared." I whispered.

"You can say no."

"But you know as well as I do that I'm not."

"Good," he whispered before brushing his lips gently across mine. I caught my breath because I wasn't expecting it. I was expecting the intense passion. Instead he was going to kiss me like he did at the opening. He brushed his mouth against mine several times teasing me just a little each time. Sometimes his tongue would dart gently in and out. It was several minutes before the kiss began to deepen. I kept wanting to push it but he kept pulling back which in itself became such a tease. I knew it was a severe exercise of control as he sucked my lower lip and explored the contours of my mouth. Even more so as he allowed me to do the same. The only touch was when his hands entwined in my hair, which he used to control the kiss. It was sublime. This was much more seductive and alluring than anything that had occurred between us before.

I was completely out of my depth with this. I wanted him so badly and it was a want that I knew was going to be more than just for one night. I wanted all of him. He was immortal. I was not and I would never be happy if I became a vampire. I would grow old and he would leave me. I just knew it and I would die from the heartbreak. I focused on my last victims. If I retired from consulting, Jared would ensure I never want for anything. Even my grandmother couldn't have argued against it. But my victims may not see justice. Detective Anderson said I would still consult but people get hurt, they die, and I would be done if something happened to him. He still had a slight limp from Ivan.

Jared broke his kiss from me and said hoarsely, "Stop thinking, lass."

I suddenly became so furious and was a little terrified at how intense and quickly it hit me. It was enough to surprise me. I rarely got mad this quick. Unfortunately, it didn't stop me from saying, "Get the fuck out then."

Jared sat there calmly, "I don't think so."

"Excuse me?"

"I have a full half hour to spend kissing you and that is my intention. I ken you're angry but that is not my fault. I spoke the truth as I see it and apparently, I have hit a nerve or you would not be quite so pissed off with me."

"I hate you," I said meaning every word.

"You hate me right this second, aye. But you don't truly hate me. There is a fine line between love and hate." He stood up suddenly, "I think I will leave you for now but I will be back. I will kiss you and I would try not to avoid it if I were you." He turned and walked out. I sat down weakly on the couch and then I got up because he had spent too much time kissing me there.

I didn't know what to do. Trust was not one of my strong points and yet he seemed to demand that I trust him.

Chapter Nineteen

I recognized it as a dream the minute I found my awareness of it. I was home and I had just turned eighteen. In this case though I was watching and observing. I couldn't help myself though and called out "Granny?" and for one brief moment I thought she was turning to answer me but then she walked to the stove to get a pot of water for tea.

That's what we did every afternoon. We would have tea together as she would question me ruthlessly about the monsters. "We need to talk, dearie," she began. I didn't know what to say but my eighteen-year-old self-listened.

"About what?" I asked.

"I'm old. Too old really. I think the locals fear me or else I would have had a hard time keeping you. I'm ninety-four years old after all."

"I didn't realize you were so far up there."

"I know but I am. I'm dying, Cassandra, and there is no use in saving me. In fact, I don't want to be saved. If you were younger, I would fight it. But you are eighteen now. I have done my best by you and the Gods have answered my prayers to live long enough to raise you."

I was so stunned that I didn't know what to say. I finally blurted, "But from what?"

"Cancer I suspect. There is a mass. It gets bigger each week. But more to the point I can feel it eating my body. I do not have much longer."

"But you need to go to the doctor!"

"So they can pump me up with drugs, make me sicker than I already am? I think not. I've lived a very long and full life. It's my time. You will graduate next month and we need to discuss your future."

"But my future is to belong with you, Granny," I cried.

"Your present is to belong here with me. Your future is something else. The Supreme Court is going to rule to make the monsters legal. The world is not prepared for the crimes that come from that popular sector. I think you should be a consultant. You're gifted. You could solve the crimes based on your gifts. I raised you not to go to college but to be able to fend for yourself using the gifts that you were born with. You are the most gifted this family has seen in perhaps centuries, if ever."

I bit my lip. "When do I have to leave then?"

"Once I am gone. Which I do not think will be too much longer."

I cried and she merely poured my tea. "Do not cry for me. I merely complete my circle. I was born. I lived. I will die. Eventually I will be reborn. I think I would like a rosebush planted on my grave."

A swirl of mist changed the scenes and I was at the library tutoring Mark Reese. He was the football captain and he needed to improve his grades desperately or he was in danger of losing his football scholarship. His father was actually paying me to tutor since I was top in the class for English and the teacher suggested it. It wasn't much but it was money.

"You know, you're quite pretty Sandie," I looked up from correcting his paper. I remember my teenage heart pitter and patter when he was nearby. Of course, that went for every girl in a hundred-mile radius. You had to be a dead stick not to notice him and even then, I wouldn't have placed any wagers in favor of the stick staying dead. I was realistic though. I was not his type and I knew it. "I think that if you paid more attention to your writing and less looking at me, you might be able to get your scholarship."

"Nah. My Dad is paying you to write my papers for me." He said arrogantly. And that was the problem with him. He was arrogant with a smirk. Ultimately, he was right. At least he gave me something to work with. "So where are you going to school, Sandie?"

"My name is Cassandra and I'm not."

"Why not? You are the smartest girl in school."

"Granny is sick and dying. I'm going to remain here until she is gone. She thinks it will be before the end of summer, though."

"But you still could go to college."

"I have other things to do."

"Like be a witch?"

"I'm not a witch."

"Everyone knows your grandmother is one and that she raised you to be one too."

"You better hush your mouth about her and me," my teenage self said furiously and I quietly wanted to applaud her. I might have had my faults but at least I had some of my priorities straight.

"Or what?"

"I'll give the money back to your father and tell him you deserve to fail and all the money in the world will not make me help you."

He turned a sheet of white, "You wouldn't," he said horrified.

"Don't you dare try me."

"Fine. Forget what I said."

"I will try very hard; I just hope it doesn't distract me as I work on your papers."

"Was I right? She's a witch and, so are you?"

"We're not witches. We don't fly around on broomsticks or any of that. We just have a deep respect for our world around us. Is that so wrong?"

"I don't know, you tell me."

"You're really a turd."

"I like you. You don't bullshit me. You're the only girl in the school who will call me a turd."

"And people say I'm cracked," I muttered.

The mist swirled again and I knew what was going on and I didn't like it a bit. "I'd like out of this dream." My response was my teenage self skipping through the woods followed by Mark. It was summer and I had graduated at this point. He had started to come by every day.

I had thought it was strange at the time and watching it again I should have paid closer to my instincts. I was caught up though. He was kissing me which of course lead to other things. I was starting to visualize having a normal life that did not involve monsters. One that would involve college and normal things. Granny was deeply concerned but she was sicker and sicker. She had me going out on a regular basis to forage for herbs to help make her comfortable.

The swirling mist again appeared and I saw Mark standing before my teenage self. I closed my eyes. I didn't need to remember this day.

"I want to see you unclothed, Sandie."

"It's best not to."

"Why? I don't understand."

"It's a long explanation. It's almost over for Granny. I would rather not discuss it."

"Please? I know it has to be your back that you are hiding."

"How would you know?"

"Because you always hide it. Nobody has ever seen your naked back. When my hands go to your back, you move them."

"It's horrible."

"I play football. How bad can it be?"

"Pretty awful but fine."

I turned my back and lifted my shirt.

Dreaming this as an observer was unique because I got to see his look of horror before he threw up. When I turned around he fled.

Granny never said a word about it until the end. When she did she said, "It's for the best dearie. Your destiny is not to molder in this small town. It is to get out into the world."

She died and I was left to make the arrangements that were necessary. It was the first time I had spoken to my father who asked what I was going to do. I told him to consult which he grunted. Whether it was in approval or not, I didn't bother asking. It had been a few days after the funeral when I had finished cleaning up the cottage and was shutting it down when someone knocked on the door.

It was Mark's Dad. He shifted a little uncomfortably. "I'm sorry for your loss."

"Thank you."

"She was always a little odd. Used to terrify me as a boy."

"She did have a way about her," my teenage self-admitted.

"I don't know if I should thank you or apologize to you."

"What do you mean?"

"I know that Mark was coming here on a very regular basis and then he stopped."

"It's nothing," I had said hollowly.

"He said something about your back. I'm sorry about the wager."

"What wager?"

"You didn't know?"

"Evidently. What wager?"

"There was a wager about why you kept your back hidden. Because I hired you to tutor my son, he became the person to find out." I was proud of my teenage self. She didn't show a single sign that the news had hurt her.

"Ah. Did he win very much?"

"I'm not sure."

"Well I am sure he got what he deserved. Now if you'll excuse me, I have a great deal to finish. I'm leaving in a few days."

"Where are you going?"

"Are you going to tell him? Because I would rather not see him again."

"No, I won't tell him."

"Chicago."

"What happened if I might ask?"

"I was tortured. For one hundred nights. It nearly killed me."

"It's why she took you?"

"Yes."

"You should know that while she was not wealthy she was fairly comfortable. She left you some money to help you and as she said, "for a rainy day." As I acted as her lawyer I have everything set up for you."

I woke up with tears streaming down my face.

Chapter Twenty

I was exhausted the next morning from the dreaming. I was nursing a very large cup of coffee when Detective Anderson called.

"Cassandra, we lost him."

"Which him did you lose?"

"Sebastian, is who."

"What?!? How do you just lose him?"

"He must have snuck out during a shift change."

"How long has he been missing?"

"At least eight hours."

"Fuck! What the hell is going on with your team? This crap I expect out of Chicago with Renaldo."

"I'm not sure what is going on but I will get to the bottom of it. The nuns, they're terrified of him. In fact, it was one of them who came to us and reported him missing. They know what he is. When questioned, everyone is uncomfortable."

"So what now?" I said very ungraciously.

"Can you hunt him down?"

"No. I can't. Not from that location. I would have had a better chance from the first victim's home. The problem is he has more than one identifier. If he changes I could lose him. He has been living at the church so that makes things even more challenging because I could go around in circles before finding the correct path."

"Understood."

"We need to go public."

"We can't say he is a criminal on the run, publicly Cassandra. He has constitutional rights."

"To hell with his rights. He will kill again. If not today, then tomorrow. He's not stable."

"If we say to hell with his rights, we are no better than he is Cassandra."

"Okay you have a point. What we can say is that he is mentally ill and escaped his caregivers. That he is confused and dangerous to himself and possibly others so if he is found don't approach him for your own safety."

"Brilliant. I'll have to get clearance but it might work."

"Does anyone have any clue at where he might have gone?"

"The nuns don't. I've questioned them twice Cassandra. You should tell Jared, though."

"Would you call Jared and tell him about it instead of me?"

"I can make the call, but are you okay? Why are you avoiding him?"

"It's complicated."

"As if anything to do with Jared is simple," he snorted. "He made a move on you last night, didn't he?"

"Did you know he was going to?"

"Well yeah, though not the details. Everyone knows he was planning it, though, so don't shoot the messenger."

"Gee I'll try not to since it is everyone knowing his intentions," I said drily.

He laughed because he did have a fucked-up sense of humor.

Chapter Twenty-One

I knew I must have completely screwed up. I didn't see or hear from Jared in weeks. Valentine's Day was approaching and I wondered if he would make an appearance then or if I was universally being snubbed for life. Fortunately, I didn't have a lot of time to spend thinking about it because my classes were in full swing. We released Sebastian's information and it was a complete waste of time. All it garnered was a lot of wasted man hours chasing down leads that went nowhere.

It wasn't until the day before Valentine's Day that anything turned up. It was three in the morning and I was being woken up.

"It's three in the morning," I groaned.

"And top of the morn to you, Cassandra." Detective Anderson said cheerfully.

"You're sick. It's a wonder Melina can stand your cheerfulness"

"Oh she hates it sometimes. Then my other sterling qualities have to take over."

I snorted in disbelief at she loved his early morning cheerfulness. "You never call to just talk. Spit it out."

"I'm texting you the address. It's another bad one."

"Sebastian?"

"It looks like it. We have a live one though."

"I'll be there."

"Try not to get lost. The house is a bit hard to find."

"I'll leave in fifteen. Try to keep the press out."

"I'm not so sure that is possible."

Chapter Twenty-Two

As it turned out I didn't have to rely on my GPS, which would have just gotten me completely lost anyway. I just followed the news van. So points for the press getting me to the crime scene. Now if they could just disappear. I had some hassle at a few checkpoints because they had some rookies working. When I spotted Detective Anderson, he was awkwardly patting a petite woman with long mousy brown hair. She had a hankie that appeared to have been fished from Detective Anderson's pocket. Personally, I wouldn't have taken if I were her, but she didn't know some of Anderson's habits.

"Cassandra, I would like for you to meet Sarah. She actually encountered the crime in progress."

"He didn't kill her?"

"She heard someone scream and had dialed 9-1-1 before going inside."

"Smart girl." The woman bristled slightly for being called a girl, so I added, "it might have been the only reason you didn't die. How many bodies?"

"Four. One man, three women."

"Oh. That's interesting." I tried to say as neutrally as possible.

"Interesting!?!" The mousy haired woman shrieked suddenly. "Who the hell are you to think that this is interesting? You are despicable!" It took Anderson more than half an hour to calm her down.

"Nice one, Cassandra," Detective Anderson said grinning ear to ear.

"Who the hell is she?"

"She is your survivor. The victim is her husband and some…umm friends."

"I don't know who those women were," the woman said, sniffing into the handkerchief.

"Her name is Sarah Wilson and she is a travelling RN. She has been gone on a lengthy assignment for a month. She came back early."

"Did the bad man say anything to you?"

"Yes. He was screaming at me about where were the rest?"

"John has been out of work for a few months but he was about to find a job soon. Ironically enough he had an interview with The Endless Night ironically enough scheduled for later this week."

"You will have to tell Jared then that there is a link."

"No Cassandra… that job falls entirely on you. He's already told me that he isn't going to speak to me until you do."

"Fine," I snapped. "Let's see the bodies I suppose."

"This crime scene is different because John and the victims were naked when they were attacked. They appeared to be to be in the middle of an orgy," Detective Anderson stated.

"You're disgusting. My husband would do no such thing. They were obviously part of what happened to him," the wife shrieked.

"Ma'am…I know you want to think the best of your husband during this trying time," Detective Anderson started to say carefully. "The problem is that the evidence does not lie and there is bodily fluid that does not involve blood, guts, and gore in there. They were all on the bed at the time. You cannot gloss that over."

Finally, I decided it was more expedient to spare the woman. "This monster is a pervert. I'm sure you have figured that out from your own close encounter. I am sure he probably requested such a thing. Didn't in his last crime scene strip more than one person?"

Detective Anderson beamed and said innocently, "Why yes, you are right. Sometimes my memory slips."

"You'll get this bastard?" Sarah looked at me, her eyes wide.

"That is my number one priority," I said with feeling and that was not a lie.

When we entered the house, I understood why Detective Anderson was sure there was an orgy going on. It wasn't just simply a man with three women. It was all the bodies piled on the bed. Clothing was thrown all over the place as if in a frenzy. It looked as if they were quite busy to have even noticed an intruder. It was also to be noted that the women at least were magical in their own right.

"It's impossible again, isn't it?"

I looked at Anderson helplessly.

"Yes," I whispered, swallowing hard.

"Well, you're in luck. There is an old shed on the property with evidence that it was recently used. We think he might have been hiding out in it."

I didn't think I would be that lucky, but I was. I even picked up one more of his personalities. With so many vying for attention it was a wonder that Sebastian's original personality ever had a chance to emerge. The sucky part was that I lost the trail. Either an unknown personality took over or travelled over water. I didn't find a trace beyond the immediate area.

After I cursed a few minutes, Detective Anderson handed me my keys. "Now you get to go tell Jared. See if any of the victims were his as well so that next of kin can be notified."

I cursed some more as he walked away laughing.

Chapter Twenty-Three

With The Endless Night open, I wasn't sure what entrance to take to get in. Was I welcome to take the private entrance or should I go in publicly like everyone else? I erred on caution and took the public entrance. The place was truly amazing. Even without the spectacle of its opening it was spectacular.

It was elevating Charlotte to a level that made it competitive with larger cities like Atlanta and NYC. There was even talk of it giving a successful bid for the Summer Olympic Games now that The Endless Night was open.

I wasn't sure what I needed to do in order to get in touch with Jared directly. It turns out I didn't need to. Peter found me. "What on earth are you doing taking the public entrance?"

"Being a normal person?" I shot back. He snorted. "Fine I wasn't sure if I was allowed to use that entrance now that it was open. So, I erred on caution and went into the public one."

"Well now you know to use the private. Follow me and I will take you to him."

"Is the Endless Night doing well?"

"We're turning a profit so if you define doing well then yes we are. If you are meaning Jared, you will have to ask him yourself."

Proof that I had been at the Endless Night too many times, I started recognizing hallways as we headed to his apartments. We weren't going to his apartments though. We took a turn which again told me we were going somewhere else. "Where are we going?"

"The gym."

He opened the door and let me in. My eyes had to adjust to the light at first since it was darkened. Peter shut the door behind him and I heard a click which told me nobody else would be entering behind me. It took me a few minutes to realize Jared was alone as he punched a boxing bag. When he heard, me move he stopped and as he came closer I realized he was wearing a kilt but no shirt. Focus on what you need to do and leave suddenly became my new mantra.

"Cassandra." He nodded curtly.

"There was another slaughter."

"Yes I heard the news."

"The male victim wasn't an employee of yours but he had an interview scheduled. We have the names of three of the female victims. They were magical and D-detective Anderson wanted for you to see if they were employees."

"And why isn't he hear delivering this?"

"Because he told me that was my job."

He became eerily still. "You have performed your duties as always admirably. You can go now."

I couldn't help but flinch at the dismissal. "Jared, please, don't be this way?"

"This way? How can I be any other way?"

"I don't like this version of you."

"I am a man, Cassandra!" He suddenly shouted with his back turned. Then quietly, "And I am also a monster. I need to accept that you will only see the later. You don't want the man."

I was stunned for a moment that this is what he thought. My problem was that I was all too aware he was a man. That I was resisting because he was a monster and that I couldn't see him as anything else was ludicrous.

He started to walk away and I ran after him putting my hand on his back for him to whirl around, "Don't touch me, Cassandra James!"

I was instantly furious. "Then don't walk away when I have something to say to you."

"What on earth could you say?" He asked coldly and I suppressed the urge to flinch.

"You're so fucking arrogant. You know that? You don't see what this could do to me professionally because you don't have anything to lose. I have everything to lose. My jobs, my reputation. Everything! All that I have worked so hard and accomplished could just go away. Oh, I know Detective Anderson said that he would always make sure I had consulting to do. However, the one thing I have learned is people die. Even you. What would happen to me if something bigger and meaner came after you and killed you? What about Detective Anderson? He's definitely more fragile than either of us! I don't know how to be anything other than Cassandra James, paranormal expert."

"Excuses. You use that brilliant mind of yours on reasons why." He turned and started punching the bag viciously again.

"Of course I do," I called out. "I don't want to be hurt and you could hurt me worse than anyone!" He stopped and decided in for a penny, in for a pound. "His name was Mark. He was a horrible boy to me. He was always teasing and he was a complete jock. His family had m-money too. At least for my area. His Dad was an attorney.

His problem was that everything was handed to him on a silver platter. His father hired me his senior year to tutor him when it looked like he wouldn't get a scholarship. I was the best in my class. Tutoring him meant spending time with him pretending to teach him when in reality I was really writing his papers for him."

"Naturally."

"Well a funny thing happened. He stopped being such a turd and became an alright guy during our times together. I f-fell in love with him and I thought he felt the same to me. He certainly said it. We m-made love but he never saw me fully naked. He never saw my back. Nobody did. People every now and then caught a glimpse but never more than a fraction of a second and not the whole thing.

That was a mistake. If I had allowed my back to be seen, it wouldn't have become such a source of curiosity. So, rumors of course abounded. He pushed for me to show him and I didn't. He finally managed to talk me into it just weeks before he was to leave. He v-vomited at the sight and called me a f-freak." By this point I was fully crying but didn't care. I had to make him understand somehow.

"I never saw him again. My Granny died a few weeks later and his f-father came by and explained it had been a wager. First my f-father, then him. After him wasn't any b-better. So forgive me if I am more than a little leery of men."

I was looking at him hoping he would understand but not sure if he did or would. When he started walking away I was sure I was going to die on the spot. I closed my eyes because I couldn't bear the sight of it. I couldn't explain when he had become so important to me but I knew I wanted to die a thousand deaths or worse, repeat my hundred nights over again before I could watch him leave me.

"Oh lass," I heard him breathe in my ear as I felt him pick me up. "You thought I was leaving you anyway? Shhh… I will never leave you."

I wasn't sure where he was taking me but I lacked the strength to resist him so it didn't matter. I just closed my eyes and enjoyed the feel of being in his presence. I knew eventually where he took me because he laid me down on a bed that was scented with lavender. "I'm such an ugly crier," I said thickly when I opened my eyes. "I always envied girls who could cry prettily."

"No lass you aren't an ugly crier. You are sublimely beautiful and those girls I would question how truthful their tears were. Your shirt is rather damp though." My mouth went dry as I realized he was shirtless. I also clearly remembered an interview Jared gave in which he was asked what he wore under his kilt. He told the interviewer he never wore anything under his kilt.

"You blush. What thoughts are you thinking?" I could feel my ears prickle from my blushing. He continued, "I can only guess. It must be something wildly inappropriate."

I couldn't help but laugh. "You have no idea."

"Actually, lass, my problem is having all sorts of ideas. I want badly to seduce you."

"Well you have a right to try," I said softly.

"Is that an invitation?"

"Maybe," I whispered softly.

He reached up and cupped my face with his hand, caressing my cheek. It felt as though he was able to read my soul in that touch. He tipped my head back and brushed his lips softly against mine. "Do you want to know what I thought the first time I saw you? I lost all respect for Renaldo in Chicago. He prides himself in his women. He even uses them to keep score over his rivals." He brushed his lips against mine again making me ache more.

"Yet he was desperate to get rid of you and you are one of greatest beauties that I have ever seen in my existence." It's impossible not to internally exult over such a statement. He deepened the kiss so my internal celebration was cut short and replaced with the ache to get closer to him. I marveled at how badly I wanted him just from a kiss.

I was burning up and it was me who pulled back from the kiss reluctantly. I pulled my shirt off. His eyes widened momentarily from surprise before filling with heat at what I had done. "Are you more comfortable now, lass?"

"Not quite," and I reached to start undoing the front clasps of my bra. His hands quickly were over mine stopping me. "Wait, allow me," he said roughly.

The back of his fingers brushed the swell of my bosom. My breasts felt heavy, full, and they ached to be touched and he was teasing. When all the clasps were undone, he bent his and with his teeth he pulled the cloth covering my right breast free. I was totally unprepared when his tongue darted out and quickly licked my right nipple and suddenly uncover my left breast and licked my left nipple.

He cupped my breasts, one in each hand and said almost to himself, "I am going to have so much fun with these."

And he did. He alternated between my breasts by first licking my nipple and then sucking. Even though I knew what he was going to do I couldn't help but gasp a little each time and I ached between my legs. I wondered if it was even possible to orgasm from what he was doing to me and my breasts. If it was possible, he was going to be the one to prove the theory.

Suddenly he stopped and gave me a wicked look. "Cassandra, lass, am I succeeding in seducing you?"

I don't know where it came from but I looked up at him and said, "I think you should try harder."

He threw back his head and laughed. When he stopped laughing his eyes glittered dangerously, "Don't say you didn't ask for it, Cassandra." I swallowed but my mouth had gone dry. He began with trailing kisses between the valley of my breasts.

"How low do I go?" he murmured almost to himself. By the time I could get my wits together to respond his tongue was licking my belly button of all places. I had no idea that could be a pleasure point. Dear Gods I was on fire and only he could quench it.

In one deft movement he slid my skirt and panties off my body. I was impressed with the technique. He had my legs spread and I had an attack of self-consciousness. A thought that fled the second I felt his fingers brush against my curls and I gasped. I gasped again when he kissed my left and right inner thighs. I held my breath when I felt his nose against my sex and I literally grasped the sheets and let out a moan so loud that I blushed the first time his tongue came in contact with me.

"You do not have to do that." I said on my next breath.

"But I want to taste you. Mmmmmm…. You are delicious.

"But…" and I lost my train of thought because one long finger had entered me to be followed by a second. There are arguments among scientists that the G-spot does not exist. Let me assure you that it exists and Jared knew exactly where to find it. I was so close.

"Jared…. please."

"Please what?"

"Take me." He suddenly went still and I wanted to cry for him not to stop.

"Do you have any idea what you just asked? Are you sure?"

I wanted to scream in frustration. "Yes I am sure."

"I could not bear having you now and later for you to turn me away with regret."

I bit my lower lip and thought for a moment. I could stop now and be satisfied. I could even pretend it never happened even. I didn't want to, though. For better or worse I think my destiny, whatever it is was to be, was entwined with Jared.

"Chopin is quoted in saying, 'It is dreadful when something weighs on your mind, not to have a soul to unburden yourself to. You know what I mean. I tell my piano the things I used to tell you.' I always thought it rather sad because of this dreadful loneliness that ate at him. I know that loneliness of not having a single soul to unburden my soul to. To share my sadness but also my joys. The question I ask you is are you prepared to be that person? Because I'll be honest. I don't come with some baggage. I come with a full set of matching luggage."

"I just have one question."

"Yes?"

"What color is the luggage?"

I laughed. "Smarty."

"Aye, lass." He got up gracefully and reached to the belt buckles on the side of his kilt. I watched him slowly as he undid the buckles. He paused for just a moment to make sure he had my undivided attention before letting go…. and the kilt dropped. I let out my breath realizing that I was holding it.

For an instance, I didn't know what to do. He was so…… "Did I stun you speechless lass?"

I couldn't help but laugh shakily. "N-no. Are you sure it will fit?"

He laughed before saying seriously, "I have never had a problem."

He was on top of me kissing me passionately again and I ached for him terribly. I could feel him against me, teasing me with the possibility that he could enter me at any point if he so chose. I kept arching my hips so that he could and he kept deftly moving out of the way so that all I got was a serious tease but no satisfaction.

"Dear Gods, Jared. Will you not just enter me already?" I groaned with frustration and the bloody man laughed. I could feel him shaking against me with laughter which didn't improve the situation. In fact, it made it infinitely worse. Finally, he said, "Why did you not say so sooner?"

Before I could retort he flipped over on his back bringing me with him and in one smooth movement he slowly began to enter me. It was at that moment that I realized I was utterly unprepared. I had of course had sexual encounters but they were brief and very lack luster. Even more pointedly, they had apparently been rather small men in the penis department. Jared at least gave me a few moments to try to adjust.

Even after that, though, I wasn't quite prepared to move. It felt fantastic and it hurt just a bit at first before feeling incredible again. Jared moved slowly in and out at a pace that eventually was just as frustrating as before. He held me still as he moved his hips down and back up. "Jared, I think it might be better if I am on the bottom this time."

He had us flipped back so smoothly that it was supernatural. I was glad to know that his breathing was as heavy and as ragged as mine. He kept a steady pace despite my efforts to change it. I was so close."

"Let it go, lass." I fell off the edge and I was conscious just enough to hear Jared. "Mo bhean dubh álainn , tá mé leatsa ." He cried out his own orgasm and was still for a moment before disengaging. He pulled me next to him.

"What did you say? You were speaking another language," I asked softly.

"I said, my beautiful lass, I am yours."

I wasn't sure what to say to that. I felt pleased but a little uncomfortable too.

"Cassandra," Jared said stroking my face. "You don't need to say anything. What I am going to have to do is go down for a few hours. Will you be okay alone tonight?"

"Yes I will be fine. Jared, I don't understand all of my feelings for you but I do know that I like you a great deal."

He kissed me gently and we just laid there. Him holding me. I must have fallen asleep because when I rolled over he was gone. If I weren't a little sore from him, I would have thought it a dream. I closed my eyes and fell back asleep.

Chapter Twenty-Four

My cell phone was ringing and I groaned because I didn't want to pick up. It was my regular ring too so it wasn't Anderson or anyone important. Finally, I heard someone distantly say, "Cassandra James's phone." Silence. "I can't wake her up she is asleep," more silence, "I beg your pardon. I will let her know you called when she wakes up."

Who on earth would be calling me? I sat up and couldn't help but blush a little as I felt the tell-tell sensation of having thoroughly been made love to. I walked out of the bedroom into the living room area. It was difficult for me to put all the names and faces to those at The Endless Night, but him, I recognized because he regularly assisted Jared. "Good Afternoon, Cassandra. Jared should be joining you shortly. In the meantime, would you like something to eat?"

My stomach rumbled. "Yes. A grilled cheese sandwich if possible?"

"A good choice. Oh, I did answer your phone earlier. I wouldn't normally do so but it kept ringing. Abigail Cummings called and spoke about some sort of fundraising event."

My heart sank. Privately, I had hoped perhaps I could see about just staying the rest of the day. This was a rare event that got school alumni and other donors together to create scholarships for students in need. Since two of my own program students received scholarships I had no choice but to say yes.

"I will call her back." I reluctantly dialed the number.

"Cassandra?"

"Yes. It's me."

"Thank God! I wanted to make sure that even with this investigation going on you wouldn't find a reason to miss this."

"So far no excuses." I said ungraciously.

"Don't find any. I will see you at 7. Oh, and who was that man that answered the phone? A boyfriend perhaps?"

"Not a boyfriend. I will see you at the party. Goodbye."

"Goodbye," she said with resignation.

It was at this point that Jared walked in and I suddenly got nervous. I wasn't sure what I was supposed to do. Get up and run to him, stay put and pretend nothing happened? "Nothing like the morning after awkwardness is there?" He finally said. I sighed gratefully and smiled. "I completely agree. It's different now."

"Last night…it does not put you under any obligation to repeat it."

"Pity, here I wanted to repeat it again and again," smiling at his look of shock. "But," I couldn't help adding, "no pressure. I would hate for you to feel like you have to keep being with me because of last night."

He leaned down and tucked a wisp of my hair behind my ear, before whispering, "I think that after you are done, that a bath would be in order."

I repressed a grin. "Perhaps."

"Perhaps what?"

"It depends on the company."

"So are you saying that you would like company? Me by chance?"

"Perhaps," I couldn't help but smile this time.

"I think all of the perhaps are really resounding yes answers."

"You are thinking correctly. What time is it?"

Jared frowned. "It's almost four in the afternoon. Why?"

"Shit! I've got to go."

"Where?"

"There is a fundraiser and I have been pressed to make an appearance."

"Why don't you skip it and I will make generous donations."

"Tempting, but Elizabeth will have me skewered if I did it that way."

"Then can I accompany you?"

I bit my lip because I knew this was going to start getting complicated immediately.

"Don't take this wrong. I don't have regrets. I've made a decision and I fully intend to explore it. However, this is going to potentially cost me everything. I want us to have the opportunity to be us before the shit hits the fan."

Jared took a deep breath. "I understand. However, if it is the fundraiser for the college I should let you know that I received an invitation."

I bit my lip. "Come but we must be seen arriving and leaving separately."

"Done." I felt awkward with the sudden silence so I did the only thing I could think of. I was so used to resisting the compulsion to touch Jared. Since he was so close I put my arms around him. I felt him pulse in surprise and when he embraced me back I could breathe again.

Chapter Twenty-Five

I am not typically an envious person. I couldn't care less what kind of money Jared would have and while I am brutally honest, I have to accept that one of the major points of him that make me uncomfortable is that he is insanely rich. However, I didn't care for cars or any of that. I loved his bath tub and it was massively embarrassing. I had suspicions that he knew that it was as seductive to me as the sirens of mythology to sailors.

My grandmother was a big believer in efficiency and that cleanliness was akin to Godliness. She saw baths as pointless because in her view you were just moving the dirt around. How can you get clean in the same water as the dirt? As a result, I only got a handful of baths and a multitude of showers. Some would find it hilarious that vampires are big on baths and indoor plumbing. After all the bacteria, parasites, and fungus that would cause us to smell do not grow on vampires. However, as it was pointed out to me, while vampires might not stink they do get dirty. It was also pointed out to me that baths still feel good to them.

I was incredibly nervous as I stood with water up to my waist in his oversized bathtub. Nervous because this was all new to me, he could see my scars and was not repulsed by them, and even more surprisingly, he found me desirable. Nervous because what if I wasn't going to be enough for him. He wasn't a monk so it had to be reasoned that there were quite a number of women before me. My back was turned away from the door because I was afraid I would squeal like some of his crazy fans when I saw him naked. I honestly was shocked that I didn't squeal or giggle like I was fourteen last night.

I heard the door open and I knew he was there. He didn't have to say anything. I could always feel him. I fought the urge to sink into the water and hide my back. I didn't realize I was holding my breath when he said, "You are so beautiful, Cassandra." I could feel my ears burn from blushing.

I heard him enter the bath and I waited for him to touch me. When he did it was a gentle hand on my shoulder before I felt his breath on the nape of my neck before he kissed me there gently. I pressed back to revel in the touch.

He kissed a trail down my spine. "Your backside is beautiful. Your scars…they are beautiful to me. They show to me a courageous woman who has survived."

I could feel myself blush and for the first time since I saw fully what was on my back, I felt pretty and was at peace with them. His hands trailed from my shoulders and cupped my behind underneath the water before moving to the front of my thighs and upwards. When he cupped my breasts with one in each hand I couldn't help but moan just a little.

"You like that lass?" He murmured huskily in my ear.

"Yes," I said softly.

"Pity you have a party or I would worship them for hours."

I couldn't even begin to fathom it. I closed my eyes and just felt until he stopped and I could feel goosebumps form without the warm of his mouth on them. I felt the water move as he moved away. When I turned around to find out what he was doing I saw him getting a large poofy sponge.

"What are you doing?"

"We don't have all night, lass. You have your party to go to. I have to get ready for it too. I am going to bathe you. Every. Last. Inch."

I sucked my breath in as my heart went wild, my stomach flipped in glee, and things in my nether region tightened in anticipation. Just simply, wow. Unfortunately, or perhaps fortunately, he knew exactly what he was doing. I couldn't make up my mind. To be overjoyed or a little uneasy.

He had me sit on the edge of the tub. I was painfully aware that he didn't have a single stitch of clothing on. I admired how comfortable he was. I doubt I would be able to move around like he did even if I had two thousand years to practice. The first touch of the sponge surprised me.

It was warm and it seemed that Jared had taken my love of Lavender scented sheets to incorporating it into my soap as well. "Relax lass," he murmured softly.

"That is so not happening Jared. Not too many women in the world can boast that she is receiving a bath by the winner of Sexiest Undead. He groaned. "Don't remind me of that ridiculous title."

"But I rather like it."

"Shh. Just enjoy your bath."

I hushed but not because of his orders. His was swirling the sponge around my breasts. I was sure that I was going to go down in history as the woman with the cleanest boobies. If I died from pleasure, which I was pretty sure was going to happen, I could picture the paramedics commenting on how extraordinarily clean they were. This would be their commentary. "Did she die from a vampire bite?" one would ask. "I don't think so…. her boobs are awfully clean though."

I didn't die but I was close. Then he began paying close attention to my legs. I didn't understand how I could be hot and cold at the same time. Nor did I have any idea how arousing soap suds sliding down my body could be until it was happening.

I was so distracted by all the other sensations that I shrieked from surprise when he spread my legs and deftly pushed past my curls with his tongue and laved me. Dear Gods…. I almost came apart the first stroke and I did the second. He didn't stop. He would stop just long enough for me to come back from over the edge just to push me right back over. I lost count of how many times before he slid me into the water and onto his erection.

I don't know what happened next. I felt my orgasm. Jared was shaking against me. And I fell. I couldn't describe it. I didn't fall into the darkness though as if I passed out. I fell into this golden light that was comforting and powerful.

Chapter Twenty-Six

I woke up surrounded by lavender scented sheets. Jared was fully dressed with the exception of his shirt open and he was pacing back and forth. His officers were there as well which I didn't understand. "Jared?"

He stopped and came over. "Are you alright?"

"Yes. Why? What happened?"

"You don't know?"

"Know. I know I must have passed out but into this golden light. It was weird."

"Well you did pass out but it was more than that…," Jared began. The fact that even he seemed concerned made me even more nervous.

"You're scaring me. Just tell me what happened."

And for his credit he blushed. It might go down as the first-time Jared MacAllistair blushed since he was a young boy. I didn't even know it was even possible for vampires to blush.

"The light came from you. It was more than a little powerful. It lifted you up in the air. You came down into the water. It seems it was more of a magical glow."

"And…"

"Well your back had a bit of a transformation." Peter finally said briskly.

I know I was giving a confused look. "What kind?"

"They're gone, lass." Jared finally said.

"Gone?"

"The scars. Whatever the hell happened, it healed all your back. In its place, there is something new."

"Everyone except Jared, please get out. I want to see this for myself."

"It's rather beautiful," Naomi inserted as she closed the door after her. I looked doubtfully at Jared. "I really glowed?"

"You really glowed."

"And the scars really are gone?"

"It's nothing like I have ever seen before."

"Well, I guess I have to see."

I got up and walked over to the closet that had mirrors. I gasped. They were really gone and I felt oddly bereft. In its place a beautiful design of a multicolored tree. It seemed to be swaying in the wind. "Holy shit."

"Exactly."

"Naomi is right though. It's rather pretty. What time is it?"

"It's a quarter after 5. Peter brought up a dress from one of the stores. Jimmy will drive you in a car that isn't known to be one of mine. I'll bring the keys to your car and it will be in place."

I was so startled about the loss of the scars that I didn't know what to do. I felt oddly robbed and blessed somehow. I wish I could talk to my grandmother. She seemed to know everything. She would have told me what this was.

I didn't realize I was crying until Jared said softly, "Please don't cry lass."

I sniffled, "It's stupid. I hated those scars for so long that I grew to accept them and now they are gone I feel like I've been robbed of something that was a part of me."

"Do you really have to attend this gala?"

"I do. The head of the school will have my head if I don't show up."

"I'll send a makeup artist up to you so that you look your best."

Normally, I would argue but with everything that was going on I just accepted. I was with him after all. I decided to commit to a relationship. I wouldn't call him a boyfriend because that just sounded so juvenile. You have boyfriends when you are twelve. However, he was definitely special.

Chapter Twenty-Seven

The room was hot and stuffy. You almost could not breathe and I didn't feel all that well. To top it all off there were a few who had on perfume so strong that you might have thought they had bathed in it. It made me want to send them an etiquette book by Ms. Manners with her rule that says that your scent should not occupy any space that you yourself do not currently occupy. With the page highlighted and bookmarked.

Jared had not arrived yet. I was starting to wonder if he was going to show up. I heard a rustle in the crowd. I knew it was him. Then I heard, "I thought he was into Cassandra James?"

"Who are they?"

I cocked my head to listen to more. He brought someone with him? That was unusual for his standards.

The crowd seemed to part around him and he seemed to be looking for me. I was a little outraged because he was not supposed to make us public just now. When I saw, who was on his arm I tried not to laugh. Melina and Naomi. They were both stunning of course. I wondered how Detective Anderson was going to take the rumors of Melina or Peter about Naomi.

Jared was wearing what was becoming my favorite kilt, his black leather. He was in black tie formal and my heart skipped several beats. When he arrived, he gave me a courtly bow. With horror, I realized what he was going to do. Renaldo had to do it once with me and I was thoroughly unsettled by it. "I, Jared, Vampire King of Charlotte, do formally present myself to you, Cassandra James, paranormal expert. Let it be known that we are friends. If anyone dares to harm you, it will be the same as harming me." I swallowed hard and curtsied. "I, Cassandra James, paranormal expert, accept your offer of protection." He turned around and began making rounds as if nothing happened.

It was nearly an hour later when Melina and I bumped into each other. "Does Detective Anderson know you're out tonight?"

"He does. He wasn't very thrilled about it but understood. Besides he and Jared have an understanding."

"What kind of understanding?" I asked curiously.

"Well it is all very Neanderthal!" Melina said, rolling her eyes. "If Jared approaches me inappropriately, Detective Anderson will have no choice but to shoot him."

"He does realize that is nearly impossible, right?"

"Well not so impossible when Jared agreed with negotiations to stand still. It's all stupid. Jared has never touched me inappropriately. He never will. So, the whole point is moot. However, all because Anderson would not be able to kill Jared, the point would be if Jared were shot it would still hurt. Even if not for long." She said that just a tad smugly.

"You enjoy the idea that Anderson behaved like a Neanderthal as you call it, don't you?"

"Absolutely. It shows that he loves me and is willing to die for me. Jared would be more than capable of making him disappear." We ended up separated again by our individual demands. I was definitely not feeling well. My head was swimming from everything that had been going on. Then there was what happened earlier.

I couldn't describe what had happened. Okay I could describe it, but there was something more going on than that I had a super great orgasm. Also, it seemed that no matter where I turned I would catch Jared's eye. He was an absolute hit. Elizabeth already knew this was the best fundraiser they had ever had. My head was swimming and I realized I absolutely had to get outside. I don't know who it was but they had a perfume so pervasive that I could taste it and my head was absolutely aching and I could feel a massive migraine coming on.

Out of desperation I sought an exit to fresh air. I found one and took several deep breaths of the clear air. My head suddenly started to clear. I looked out onto the city that was absolutely beautiful. I loved Charlotte, I suddenly realized. There was something about this city that appealed to my deepest senses.

It was one of those moments that was surreal. I was looking down watching the people distracted by the limo pulling up. I recognized Jimmy hopping out. Then Jared stepped out and for some reason just like tonight he looked up. It was then that I suddenly felt the energy of him, the shapeshifter roaring at me. He slammed into me and sent me falling.

Falling from a building does not give you much to think about but the one thought that was in my head was how much I was going to miss Jared. The second thought was that it was taking longer than it ought to.

"Holy Jesus, Jared," I heard Naomi breath and I opened my eyes. It took a few minutes to register but I was suspended about a foot in the air. It also didn't take a genius to realize that it was Jared. I could see the look of awe on both Naomi and Melina's face.

Jared was slightly stunned. He seemed to shake it off. "This is what is going to happen. Jimmy move the car up so that we have more privacy. Cassandra, I am putting my arms underneath and I will let go so that you fall into them. I will immediately put you in the car. Naomi when Cassandra is in the car with me go inside and make her excuses. Tell them that she had a stomach virus and that Melina is driving her home. Melina take Cassandra's car and take it to Detective Anderson's. Then bring him back to the Endless Night. Naomi once we are back at the Endless Night, get the officers together."

By the time Jared was done talking, Jimmy was there and it was action. It gave me a whole new appreciation of Jared and his staff. When I was safely in the limo and Naomi and Melina were off fulfilling their tasks, I was alone with Jared, who held me close and began whispering in my ear.

"This must never get out to the public. It will put you in way too much danger if anyone knew."

My heart skipped a beat because I had never heard of a vampire being able to do something like this before. Flying yes but this no. It would elevate him without question to the most dangerous vampire in the world and perhaps ever.

"I'll never say a word to anyone about what you did."

Jared laughed softly and just a little sardonically. "Cassandra lass it isn't what I can do. It's what *you* can do. The energy that saved you didn't come from me. I was helpless to watch you fall. You gave me the energy to stop you in mid-air. I knew how to do it because I can fly. Or at least the general mechanics. I saved you because I have very keen instinct and can move rapidly with an action plan."

I was stunned. Me? He was mistaken. He had to be. "You have to be wrong Jared. I don't have an ability like that." There I said it. Now he must believe me.

"Why not? Answer me that. Why can't you have extraordinary magical abilities? You regenerate yourself as fast as any of my shape shifters. In fact, better in some aspects. You can track any source of magic and match it like a fingerprint. No... better, like DNA. That in itself is an unusual gift. It scared the hell out of Renaldo. Just a few hours ago you healed scars on your back. So, in all of that why do you think I am wrong?"

I didn't have an answer. In truth, it was wishful thinking. Wishful because it made me exactly like what I had to hunt. Because I didn't answer, Jared continued.

"You heal so well that even my best self-healer in my cats is not a match. Last year if one of my cats had the same injury you had from when you were stabbed, they would have died. To a smaller degree you helped me at the opening of The Endless Night. You are pure magic."

I had enough and was suddenly angry. "Shut up alright! Just shut the fuck up! Everything I am has somehow brought on a bone wrenching misery. I lost my home and my family. I was lucky Granny was even alive and then I watched her constantly in fear that she would keel over! You, you love being a vampire. You are so powerful not many would dare mess with you. You are surrounded by people who absolutely adore you!"

I saw the look on Jared's face and I took a step backwards. "I love being a vampire?" He asked, his voice laced with sarcasm and I took another step back. "I suppose there are aspects. I do love knowing I am one of the best in existence. I love being able to care for my people. I love knowing that I can make a positive difference in the world, even. It's not a barrel of laughs. I hate knowing that every single one of my people will grow old and die and I will not. I hate watching every single one of the people I am close to die. I have buried five companions in two thousand years. 5 women whom I have loved with every fiber of my being and I am prepared to do it a sixth time with you. I could keep them safe. They never wanted for anything. Just as I draw breath you will never want for anything. The only thing I couldn't or wouldn't if you choose to look at it that way was save them from time. Just as I will with you, I watched them grow old and die. Maybe though, just maybe that whatever this magic is….it will be such that I won't lose you in a mere blink of the eye like I did them."

I didn't know what to say to make things right other than to put my hand into his. Before I could say something, we arrived back to The Endless Night.

Chapter Twenty-Eight

I heard Detective Anderson complain, "Melina my dear. Could we just go back to my place? I'd rather avoid him just now. He doesn't look happy." Jared was glowering and pacing.

"You told me to bring him here so don't look at us that way." Melina said hastily.

"It's alright. You did exactly as I told you," Jared said gruffly. He was moody ever since we arrived. For some reason Melina came over to me and put her arms around me and hugged me. I felt a little better.

Jared looked at Detective Anderson whose hand kept wandering to the holster of his gun. "Cassandra James is dead."

"No offense but she looks a little alive to me."

"For now she is dead. The bastard caught her unawares and threw her off the building. Luckily, she was able to save herself."

"You helped." I interjected.

"Finally starting to admit that it might not have been all me?"

"Jared, unless you want a pink wardrobe for the rest of your life, you will just stop it right now." Melina snapped.

"I could fire you Melina." He snapped back.

"You could but you won't," she said calmly. "There won't be anyone taking the empty role and it is a calling to work for you in that capacity. The job is difficult. Besides, if left to your own devices you will look a fright. So, lay off it or choose pink or being out of fashion for a generation. If you are lucky it's a generation. It might take two to get past the story. Oh, and the Brussel sprouts will become a regular menu fixture."

Detective was looking back and forth between all of us. "Evidently I am missing out on a few things."

"Sebastian didn't bother checking to make sure Cassandra hit the ground," Jared said simply. "He thinks she is dead. So, she will be until he commits a crime that she can track. I estimate that will be soon. Also, because she is dead and the only one in the known world with her exact abilities he is guaranteed not to be careful."

Anderson was looking at me waiting for a decision. "It makes sense. I do have one question though. What's this all got to do with Brussel sprouts?"

Jared took a deep breath. "Mike you do realize you can be an annoying man?"

"It's a gift," he quipped back and suddenly all the tension in the room diffused.

"The Brussel Sprouts is because Jared can taste the food that his people eat," I added as explanation. "I gather, Melina, he doesn't care for them?"

"He hates them," Melina confirmed, her eyes sparkling with amusement.

So, the game plan was that I would be publicly pronounced dead. The story was going to stick to the facts. If anyone was watching they would have seen Jared picking me up. Jared, armed with the craftiness of Detective Anderson, obtained all the surveillance video of the area. They announced my death at a press conference and they showed the video of me falling and stopped short of showing me stop in mid-air.

It was, in a word brilliant. What nobody expected was the media shit storm that exploded around it. It ended up becoming world news as the networks picked up the story and turned it into Breaking News. I was not prepared for how surprised I was by some reactions. The first shock was when Renaldo called Jared. He yelled at Jared for half an hour and wondered how it was possible that he was better at keeping me safe. He was genuinely upset at my death. Jared had to tell him the truth. Then he said, "I always suspected." Renaldo grunted, "There is nothing to suspect."

The second shock was my father. He was threatening a religious war before he was done ranting enough for Jared to explain. He was not happy with the idea. He was downright pissed that next of kin had not been warned and was hearing it via the media. I honestly didn't think it would matter. When I explained, he said he understood. For the first time, I think he finally regretted what he had done to me.

Jared thrived in the limelight. Detective Anderson and his team. on the other hand, were nowhere near prepared for the sheer magnitude of it all. My students were struggling to deal with it and the college was scrambling because this was the last thing they had ever expected.

It was weird seeing colleagues and acquaintances giving interviews. The ones that outraged me the most were my so call friends from school. I was dozing off and on in Jared's arms wishing my grandmother was here to explain what the hell happened to me. Then an epiphany of sorts when I remembered I had everything of hers. My father wanted none of it so I put it all in secured storage.

Jared was lazily stroking my back when I said, "Jared?" I felt his hand stop. "Yes, lass?"

"My grandmother kept journals. Detailed journals. I have them in storage. Would you be willing to arrange for them to be brought here and stored?"

"Consider it done. Do you think you will find answers to what happened in the bathtub?"

"I'm not sure. Most likely not, but it's worth looking into. I honestly don't know what all is there. I never read any of them."

"Where are they located?"

"Chicago. The storage unit is under Alyssa Monroe, Greenman's Storage."

Jared laughed in delight. "Who you were drove Renaldo mad as he tried to uncover your past and he couldn't crack the code. Your father had been too good at erasing his connection to your grandmother. And it was under his nose the entire time?"

"Essentially. Though I didn't mean for it to be evasive to him. I didn't want anyone to be curious about the contents. When I was falling, you were who I was thinking about Jared. I thought about how much I would miss you."

I fell asleep to Jared singing softly ancient songs in ancient languages that had died long ago.

Chapter Twenty-Nine

What we were doing was a gamble. Detective Anderson, I learned might be a bit of a sociopath. He didn't oppose the idea because he wanted to catch him even if it cost more human life.

It was two in the morning a week after my supposed death when a very relieved and inappropriately happy Detective Anderson called. He received a call from a Sheriff Graham out of Lincolnton with a homicide that looked much like what we had been dealing with.

Anderson was particularly joyful because the family he attacked was not magical. They were a bit strange and gravitated to Goth but magic they were not. "He was sloppy with his research," Anderson said happily. Jared was more muted because of the location.

"Spill…. Jared. Lincolnton is your territory so I'm not quite understanding this."

"It's complicated, lass."

I sighed and rolled my eyes. "When is anything to do with vampires not complicated?"

"That's not entirely true," he protested.

"Spill Jared!"

"I need to call Samantha. She is the unofficial queen of Lincolnton."

I whistled low. "Now that I didn't expect."

"The territory is mine but Samantha…. everything for her is about appearance. She has been styling herself as a Queen for about fifty years."

"And you've let her?"

"She is content with just that area. She knows I am letting her and she knows who it belongs to. Hickory knows not to mess with it because it really is mine and that I allow Samantha's charade because it's convenient."

"Why do you allow it?"

"She is newish. She was turned just a little too young during the Spanish Influenza. She has spirit but no serious potential. She has a great mind though and she does manage her bit very efficiently. She thrives at being the center of attention."

"Was it one of your vampires who turned her?"

"No it was myself. She was fifteen and dying. Except she didn't want to die. One of my shapeshifters begged me to at least look at her. She was not going to survive the disease. She had spirit and was not going to go gently into the night. I didn't realize quite how young she really was but I couldn't tell her no."

"So you pretty much keep an eye out for her."

"Yes. She will love the spotlight. But I am going to have to ask her permission for you."

I know an eyebrow shot up at that.

"It's a game, Cassandra. She and I have been playing it for so long that this is just how our relationship is defined."

"Were you ever involved with her in a different way?"

"Do you mean romantically?" He asked with a grin.

"Yes."

"The answer is no. However, I did kiss her once as a favor to her. She wanted to know what it was like to be kissed properly. She did have a huge crush on me for a while but that was a long time ago."

I didn't quite understand it but I wasn't going to argue with Jared. It didn't hurt him and it seemed that Samantha was common knowledge.

Chapter Thirty

It was nearly three thirty by the time my passage was negotiated and we were heading up the 321. Jared sent Peter with me and while he didn't say anything I knew he wanted to go himself.

Something he could never do of course, but I knew he wanted to. I didn't question myself, though. I knew that I could take Sebastian on. It was just tracking him down. He wasn't expecting it.

When we arrived to the crime scene, there was a skeleton crew. Anderson had made the request. The Sheriff didn't like it but complied after he had done a double take at my presence. When I stepped out of the car, I thought he was going to faint. "I hope I get a better reaction from Sebastian when I find him." I commented blandly.

"You're alive?"

"Exactly, and now I hunt." I smiled because I knew Sebastian really had screwed up. He had picked a truly non-magical family. I had my execution sword with me and it was going to be used today.

Detective Anderson was wound up pretty tightly and looked at me anxiously. "Let's get to work. I don't think he moved far from the crime scene. He wouldn't expect a preternatural expert to be in the region yet. He might even have one more family marked."

I closed my eyes and just felt. As I opened my eyes I could feel where he had been and it was almost like a path.

I was fully prepared. I was wearing all black from head to toe. Jared had personally braided my hair and I had tucked it under a black beret and secured it with pins so that I could hunt. Before I walked away from him he whispered, "Try to come back to me in one piece."

I threw my arms around him and kissed him. "I promise."

"Peter, you need to follow but at a distance. I don't want him to smell you. Anderson stay out of this. I can't afford to be distracted. Sheriff Graham… keep your men back and can you tell me what is back that way?" I pointed where the trail was leading me.

"A barn, I think, but it's way out there."

The trail was leading me to something but until I realized that there weren't many options. I didn't want to go inside the barn because I had no idea what all was inside it. I wasn't sure what I was going to do until I heard someone scream. "Shit he has another victim."

So I decided to bring him out. It was a gamble. "Sebastian!"

I heard Peter whisper, "Cassandra what are you trying to do?"

"Trust me." I whispered. Then I shouted again, "Sebastian, you naughty boy. Come out to me. I am here waiting for you."

The barn door opened and I had my weapons ready. "You aren't real. You're d-dead." He called out. "Go away."

"Oh but I am real."

"I killed you. I p-pushed you off the building."

I almost groaned because I had the real Sebastian. I wouldn't hesitate killing the monster personalities. Him it would be harder. I was suddenly struck with an idea to see how much Father Morgan had to do with all of this.

"You saw wrong. I have a secret. Can you keep one?"

I saw the look of mistrust but curiosity warring with each other and he took an involuntary step forward. I could hear Peter suck a breath in and I knew I was going to get a tongue lashing when this was all over.

"What is the secret?"

"I don't know if I should say." He took another step forward.

"You're lying then about it." He accused almost petulantly.

"No… it's just that you will tell them." I referred to his personalities.

"I won't. I don't tell them everything, you know."

"Well…. if you are sure. I don't want them to know."

I had him hook, line, and sinker.

"Well Father Morgan, he talked to me about you."

"Did he tell you what a good boy I really am?"

"Well…. not exactly. You know Father Morgan. He has his favorites."

"How do you k-know that?"

I shrugged. "I was one of his favorites."

"You were?" He stepped closer to me. "How long did he keep you?"

I swallowed hard because I knew everything hinged on this. "I shouldn't say. You might not like it," I said softly.

"Oh please. I won't be mad. I p-promise."

"Well since you promised," I took another step closer and shifted so that my machete was in a more defensible position. "He kept me 100 Nights."

"Whoa…. you are special. He has never kept anyone longer than forty-five days."

"I have another secret."

"What is it," he almost begged as he took another step closer. I was close enough.

"I'm still his favorite. He would give anything to have me back. He told me so himself." Since that last part was the truth it rang with a truth that he could not refute.

I felt sad for him as the truth sank in. The truth that he was never going to be good enough because I was the one that got away. He blinked back tears. I was destroying him to get the monsters that were in his head. This poor man who was victimized repeatedly. I swallowed past the lump in my throat. I wasn't enjoying my job at all.

"No…I am his favorite. He has told me so. He takes care of me. He says he l-loves me. He makes sure I am cared for. Always."

"Oh Sebastian, I'm so sorry. He hates you. How do you think I was able to find you?"

I always marvel later how major events tend to slow down. When I was young, I was in a car accident and the window on my side of the door shattered. To this day I can remember the moment of impact and how each fragment of glass flew out. An accident that rationally took just a few seconds felt like an hour suspended in slow motion.

I would never forget this. It was over so quickly, but it felt like forever. He closed his eyes and a single tear fell from his left eyelash and I watched it streak down his face until it disappeared into the stubble of a day's' worth of beard growth. I saw his eyes open and they were not his but one of his twisted personalities that had taken over. I was ready and was already ducking as he reached out to strike me. His hand turning into a paw with vicious claws.

I saw my machete pierce him through the chest and I could feel the damage being inflicted as I felt it slice into him. I knew instinctively that it was a kill shot. He looked down and when he looked up the monster was gone. "C-Cassandra? Was it t-true?"

I couldn't say anything except to shake my head no. "It d-doesn't really hurt that bad you know. We are free now" He closed his eyes, fell back, and I removed my machete and swiftly cut his head off. I didn't feel any blood that flew at me. I sank down on my knees and cried.

Chapter Thirty-One

I don't know how long I sat there. I didn't look up until Detective Anderson said, "Cassandra, news reporters are just over the hill. We need to get you out of here."

I nodded numbly. I felt Peter walk beside me. I liked Peter. He didn't talk but just his presence said volumes. Unfortunately, we were spotted by a stray reporter who started screaming, "Oh my God! Isn't that Cassandra James?" Detective Anderson groaned.

"Get her out of here. She is no condition to answer questions. I'll explain it all."

I began to protest but Peter cut in, "You're covered in blood. You cannot go on TV like that."

I looked down at myself and saw that there was a large amount of blood on me so I nodded in agreement. Odd that I didn't notice it before or how I was cold. I was shivering by the time I sat down in the car. I'm not sure where it came from but a blanket almost magically appeared. I was exhausted and was falling asleep when I felt Peter patting me on the face.

"You're in shock so I can't let you go to sleep. Tell me why you decided to give Jared a break."

"It seemed pointless to keep fighting it. I am drawn to him like a moth to the flame. I am unable to change that attraction."

He didn't look all that convinced. It didn't matter if he was or not. Jared was waiting for me when I arrived. The way the breeze picked up his hair reminded me strongly of the first time I met him. With him I knew that I would not worry about him condemning me as a monster. Before he got close to me I said quietly, "With him I can be me and it will be okay."

When I approached Jared, he glanced down at me. "His I presume?"

"Yes."

He merely walked beside me until we got fully inside. It was then that he picked me up. "I have a bath waiting for you lassie."

I glanced back at Peter and raised my eyebrow to say, "See. I told you so." He shrugged his shoulders while shaking his head with wonder.

Chapter Thirty-Two

It was hours later when Jared told me. "We found a letter when we went through your grandmother's things."

"A letter?"

"Yes. It was addressed to you."

I blinked, perplexed, because she wasn't much of a letter writer. In fact, I could not recall her ever writing a letter now that I thought on it.

"I think it might be important. I'm going to leave you alone with it, okay?"

"Okay." I said, still stunned.

I recognized the handwriting on the envelope as hers so I knew it was real. What I read, however, was a bit of a surprise.

Cassandra,

If you have broken the seal to this letter, then I know that events have led you to look for deeper knowledge. That is in my final journal and it is encoded there. Below is what you need to break the code.

You are the last of us now. I am thankful every day that I have lived long enough. I was afraid when I took you in that I wouldn't have enough time. Never has time been more my mortal enemy. I feared that I would die before I could finish raising you. If I had been younger, I could have been a resource for longer like my mother was to me and as her mother was to her.

Our family is an ancient one. We are one long unbroken line from a single maternal source. We were, before even the vampire king, Jared took his first breath. We were what legends were made of. I rather suspect when all is said and done we will be again through you. I am tired and my body is weak. I have had so much to teach you that I did not express enough how precious you have been to me. The daughter I did not have or expect to have. So, fierce and brave you were. How defiantly you gazed at me when I walked into that hospital room to take you into hiding.

I quietly folded the letter up and went looking for Jared. When I found him, I said, "Here is the letter. Her last journal is coded and this letter has the key to break it."

"Do you not want to do it yourself?"

"I do…. but it will be faster if you do it." The silence between us was deafening.

"Spit it out Cassandra. You have something else to say." Jared said harshly.

"A lot has happened over the last weeks. I would like to go back to my home. I miss my own space."

His face was unreadable. "Do you want to see me again?" He asked, his voice harsh.

I realized that he was expecting me to walk out. "I would be devastated if I did not see you again. I just need a little time to myself."

"Will you bring a bodyguard?" He asked a little thickly.

"No. I will compromise. You can send one after I have a few hours to myself."

He was silent for such a long time that I suppressed the need to shift uncomfortably. "I dinna see how that would hurt," he finally said. I turned to leave. "Cassandra?"

I turned back, "Yes?"

"Dinna stay gone for too long. I would miss you if you were gone."

I swallowed hard. "I would miss you terribly too. I will be back tomorrow night if that is okay?"

He hugged me fiercely. It took all my strength to leave.

It was a quiet drive back to my place. Jimmy didn't really talk that much and I was too tired and preoccupied in my own head to do much.

There was a certain comfort to being in your own home. It was so silent too though. I had not realized how accustomed to the hum of energy and noise that was The Endless Night. I cleaned myself up with a quick shower and because I was tired I crawled into bed. A bed that just didn't feel right. Nothing felt right and it was sheer force of will that kept me from calling Jared to come and get me. I didn't know how I was going to manage keeping our relationship a secret.

It was an hour after I crawled into bed and was still blinking into the darkness when I heard the alarm beep as someone had entered the code. I figured it must be Peter so I got up. I figured I could talk it out with him.

When I stepped out of my room I was overwhelmed by a sickening sweet smell before everything went dark.

Chapter Thirty-Three

I woke up to darkness. I tried to move but I was completely bound. The sudden panic almost completely overwhelmed me. I concentrated on breathing and started counting my breaths silently in my head. I opened my eyes to realize that while it was dark it wasn't completely void of light. I knew who had me. I didn't know how he got through Jared's security system.

Jared. His name was almost painful and I knew I had to tuck it away if I was going to survive what was coming after me. I didn't have long to wait. When he limped in he was in a happy mood. "Well now! I am pleased to see that you are awake. I was almost afraid that I had overdone it with the Ether."

"Where am I?"

"Oh I think it doesn't matter where you are. What I do know is your boyfriend will never find you."

"I wouldn't make any large wagers on that."

"Alyssa, Alyssa. Defiant as ever. Now what I want to know is who on earth managed to fix your back? I went through so much effort with it. I was almost sad to see it gone."

"Almost?"

"Almost. Then I reminded myself that I wasn't exactly happy with the first and that God presented me with a blank canvas."

I kept my mouth shut. This was my worst nightmare but I had to survive it. To survive it I had to not fight so hard. To accept it, embrace it, and wait for an opportunity. He made mistakes. He was going to make another one and I would make sure I killed him.

I was almost nodding off when the first crack of the whip came. I jerked my head up.

"Good! That woke you up. I want you to pay very close attention to what I am going to do to you."

He whipped me 102 lashes. I could feel the blood dripping from my back. It fucking hurt. There was no other way to say it. When he said 100 lashes I had to correct him. "102."

"What did you say?"

"It was 102. You're getting old. You can't count the way you used to I think. You repeated 67 and 82 twice."

"Are you saying I make mistakes?"

"With all due respect given that I am the one being whipped I can assure you that you miscounted."

I wasn't prepared quite for the crack across the face with his hand. Damn did he have to hit so hard? I blinked stars before I made myself start laughing.

"Are you daft girl?"

"Perhaps. I was just thinking."

"About?"

"Jared. If I don't kill you, he will."

"I don't think Jared is looking for you. You left a note telling him it was done between the two of you."

My heart sank just a little but I didn't think something like that would work. He was too persistent. So, I did what I had to do. I counted and hoped I wasn't too weak when the time came.

He loosened me just enough that I could have feeling back in my hands before he left. As soon as I could, I started to work on my bonds. There was just a slight give when my arms were not over my head. The rope cut into my wrists but I had to work past that.

I kept struggling with flashbacks of the first time. It was getting dizzyingly disorienting. My new mantra was to get free and kill him. When I felt like it was overwhelming me I started to count again. 1…2….3….4….

How could I have been so stupid? I should have known he would try to do this again. I should have defied Jared. It might take my last breath but I was going to kill Father Sampson. I was going to kill him for myself and for Sebastian who would not have become what he had if he had not been tortured. When I see Jared again I was going to slap him too.

I liked how positive I was given that I was naked, tied up, and covered in dried blood. Dried blood that I might like to add was starting to get itchy. Father Sampson came back and I knew he was going to have "confessional" time. I was supposed to confess the sins of my past. I almost giggled because I am sure I could tell him a few things now that would make his celibate heart blush crimson.

"I would ask you what evilness you are up to but it's splashed all over the news so I don't really need to."

"Then just get on with it."

"Oh I will my dear. Don't be too anxious. I am rather curious how you healed your back like that."

"Do you really want to know?"

"Yes I rather think I do."

"Then you owe me a question."

"M'dear you are in no position to negotiate."

"Oh but I am. You want to know how I fixed the scars. I don't have to tell you and I think you have figured out that I don't give up anything while being tortured."

He stroked his chin thoughtfully. I wondered if when I was killing him that I could break each one of his fingers before I finished him off. My inner mind didn't shudder at the savagery of it. In fact, I got a resounding a round of applause at the thought.

"What is the question?" He finally asked.

"Why me?"

"Deal. I wanted you. I saw you playing in the park and recognized what you were. It was just my luck that your father recognized that you were a freak and was very easy to convince that you were possessed."

"What do you mean?"

"I recognized that you could sense the monsters. We thought about using you but you were already willful and stubborn. We knew you had to be broken to be useful."

I shook my head in disbelief. "All that for me to turn into the thing you wanted me to become."

"No. You aren't an assassin. You would be an assassin for the church. You seem to feel like they have to prove they deserve it for you to do it."

"How I healed my back was quite simple. I had an orgasm." I watched with glee as his face contorted with fear. "Apparently, it was quite a spectacular one. I even fainted," I said dryly.

"You think you are going to mock me, girl." He shouted with flecks of spittle splattering on my shoulders and face. I tried not to cringe from how unhygienic it had to be.

"I'm not mocking. Just telling you the truth. Jared went down on me, I glowed golden and when I stopped glowing the scars were gone. When you took me, we were trying to figure out what caused it but I guess we will never know."

"Went down on you?"

Damn I forgot all about the celibacy thing for just a moment. "Just Google it. It will explain it and maybe offer you videos."

He punched me square and the face. My head exploded in pain. In fact, I had to thank him for it because the next thing I felt was him slicing into my back. In reality it didn't take long. It felt like it took forever though from my point of view. I was very happy with the throbbing of my cheek. Though I did question if he didn't manage to fracture it.

I closed my eyes to start counting in my head again but my eyes flew open when I heard a loud bang outside the door to the room. Father Sampson was momentarily distracted and I made my move. I yanked back hard and even though I felt the rope bite into my wrists. The bonds broke. I'm not sure he realized the bonds had broken but he made the mistake of hesitating when he saw my hands. So, I knew it was do or die. I wasn't going to leave this room alive if I didn't give all that I had.

I spun my body around and I hit him as hard as I could. It wasn't a death blow but he was definitely hurt. He stumbled backwards grasping his head. I took one of his knives and sliced through the ropes that had my feet tied down and I got a good distance from the bastard.

My body was on fire. It took me a second to get my head together. My back still ached but adrenaline had finally kicked in. I thought very briefly about torturing him for a while but I had no idea if he would be missed so I dismissed the thought. "You must realize I'm going to kill you," I said quietly.

He lunged at me to try to take knife. I side stepped and hit him as hard as I could. "I am going to kill you for robbing my childhood. I am going to kill you for every death that is at your hands. It is over for you." I brought the blade down and sliced through his femoral artery. I didn't think I was going to torture him but that was good enough. He knew as he was trying to stop the bleeding that he was dead.

He was screaming curses until I finally said, "You are dead. Instead of screaming curses to me you might want to make things right with your God. I'm pretty sure that given what happened to Jesus, God doesn't approve of torture. But I wouldn't know. I'm just a harlot of Babylon."

He shut up. His breathing was labored and he began to shake uncontrollably. Until he finally gasped for breath one last time. He was dead and I was glad of it. He didn't exit the world gently. I heard banging but it didn't register that it would be related to me. Suddenly I heard another loud bang and several large beefy men rushed in. I immediately crouched, not thinking at all about the fact that I was naked.

They immediately turned their eyes though and I heard a slow even clap. I cringed at the voice, "Well done, Cassandra."

It was Renaldo, the Vampire King of Chicago.

Renaldo was average for height. He was handsome but not overly. His short black hair was combed back and his lime green eyes practically gleamed with amusement. He always wore the best suits money could buy. He was lethal and could order my death in the same voice that he used to compliment me. I was in no condition to fight off him and his minions.

"Oh don't look so worried, Cassandra. I'm not here to harm you. In fact, I'm supposed to be here saving you," he looked over at the body of the priest, "however it does seem like you have things well in hand." He pointed over to one of the burly men, "You. Give Cassandra your jacket. She seems to be in need of some clothing. Then go out to the car. She and I need to talk in private." I groaned internally. The last thing I wanted was to deal with Renaldo covered in blood naked.

"Yes boss." He surprisingly put the jacket gently around my shoulders.

"I'm sorry ma'am. I should have thought of this on my own." I smiled shakily and said, "Thank you."

I looked warily at Renaldo. He was being too nice. "So why are you really here?"

He sighed because it was the same game as always with him. "Like I said. I'm here to save you. Now it seems like I am just here to clean up the mess. A very interesting position for me to be in with regards to you. Positively ironic."

I looked skeptical so he finally said, "Of all the holes in the world for him to take you. It had to be my city. Jared has been frantic. They knew you were missing within two hours. Jared sent out a private alert to every vampire king and queen in the world. He contacted me privately because a private plane left and was headed to Chicago. We guessed that you might be on it."

"How many days have I b-been down here?" I really didn't want Renaldo to have heard me stammer. He didn't seem to notice it though.

"In total 5 days."

"Then what took you so long?"

"Hey don't blame me. You left a well-trained preternatural unit and your successor is almost as much of a pain in the ass as you were except not as pretty. They nabbed the guy who met the priest on an unrelated charge. I had to bail the man out just so that I could get my hands on him."

"You couldn't just make the police turn a blind eye?"

"Precisely. What is the world coming to that an honest criminal has to take legitimate measures?"

"Poor you." I said sarcastically.

"Jared was frantic. He was worried about your life and sanity in general. I wasn't." He paused and a slow smile spread across his face. "I always knew you could take a good spanking. I should have done it years ago."

I couldn't help but laugh. "He says you respect me."

"I do. You're alive, aren't you? When you came to my city I scoffed. You were this little country girl with these alleged skills. The police thought you were a joke. I thought you were one too. But you were ferocious. You were so scared during our encounters that I could taste it. Yet you never once backed down. You killed my best and I would never have guessed that would even be possible. But damn you were a righteous pain in the ass." He chuckled.

"You are his chosen now you know. It's not public but we all know it by the way he made finding you a priority."

"Chosen?"

"He's chosen you as his mate. It's a major deal among vampires and even bigger with him. I knew his last one. I was never so happy when she died. You on the other hand... you're certainly different than her."

"Different how?" I was shocked and intrigued.

"You have your own magic. You are strong in your own right. Anne made tea nervous. When she found out the truth about Jared she went crazy and Jared was fool enough to make sure she was not institutionalized. I'm glad he has someone who is more of his match than the last one."

"Why so much concern about that?"

"He made me. That is a loyalty that will never end. And through Jared you Cassandra James are my Queen. How ironic is that? My pain in the ass turned Queen. I certainly didn't see that one coming."

Because it was being all so serious I had to say something that would lighten the mood. "So how long ago did he make you?"

He threw his head back and laughed. "You know better than to ask. Especially since I know you have to know."

"I do but you can't blame a girl for wanting confirmation that she is right."

"You're dangerous."

"So what happens now?"

"We leave. I will take you back to the Ivory Tower. Jared will be here soon enough. He was en route when I found this place. My men will take care of the corpse."

We stepped out into the cold night. It was a dingy alley that the door opened out to. Renaldo changed cars twice. The last being a stretched Escalade.

His phone rang and he picked up. "Is he here?" Followed by, "I understand. Tell him to sit tight and wait."

When he hung up he looked over. "Jared is here and he will be waiting. When we arrive, I'll get out first and then you."

"So if you respected me why did you make it so damn hard?"

Renaldo shrugged. "It's what I do. We all have a purpose in life. Your purpose is to chase the bad guy. My job is to give you someone to chase." It was the most fucked up piece of logic I had ever heard, but it also made sense in its own way.

Chapter Thirty-Four

We arrived in one of the most immaculate parking garages. I could see Jared pacing. He looked the most untogether I had ever seen. Melina was there talking frantically to him. Trying to keep him calmed down I rather suspect. She looked equally disheveled. Renaldo exited first and gave a nod to Jared. Renaldo then turned and offered me his hand.

Suddenly it seemed like the world faded and while I promised to keep it together, tears sprang and I ran into his arms and sobbed quietly. When Jared put his hands on my back I flinched and he removed them quickly. As I calmed down I heard Renaldo remark, "I will never understand women. In all the time, I have known her she has never cried. She killed my best and didn't cry. She was prepared to kill my bodyguards earlier tonight if need be."

"Is the priest dead?"

"Of course," Renaldo snorted. "He didn't die pretty either by the judge of the mess. She bled him out. Which was a damn waste of good blood."

"I'm sure you can find more," Jared said sarcastically.

"I could, but the point is that the blood was utterly wasted and it's going to be a major cleanup too."

I was taken to a suite of rooms that had been set up for Jared. It was all modern. It took two tub soakings to get me clean enough for the doctor to examine me. Each time the water was changed was agony because my back burned and itched because I could feel it healing. Jared brooded the entire time but kept quiet until I sat down to a bowl of soup.

"Father Morgan said you wouldn't look for me because he planted a note telling you that I was leaving."

"I got it and it was very convincing. I almost just let you go."

"What convinced you otherwise?"

"Peter. He was adamant that you would never disappear like that. He thought your feelings were deeply genuine. I wasna thinking too clear."

"He deserves a raise. I would not simply leave like that ever."

Can I tell you something but you promise to keep eating?"

"Yes."

"We deciphered some of what your Grandmother had to say. Apparently, you are Morrigan."

"What is that?"

"The Morrigan are ancient. They are the three guises of the Goddess. Maiden, Mother, and Crone. Legend has it that during one of her Maiden forms, the Goddess fell in love with a human man. 9 months later the Goddess becomes her Mother form. The child, though while powerful and special, was very much mortal.

All the descendants of the line, which weren't very many, were always special in some way. Your Grandmother believes you are the one who will turn out to be the most gifted of them all. We thought the line went dead we thought centuries ago. Apparently, it's been alive and well. The Church hunted your ancestors even more fiercely than us. I think because your line was a visible reminder that God wasn't the only one after all."

"Jared?"

"Yes lass?"

"I think I am going to tap into my inner Scarlett O'Hara and will think about it tomorrow. Will you sleep with me?"

"Of course."

Curled up, he whispered to me, "I thought I had lost you and that I was going to have to tear the world apart."

"But you didn't lose me. I am here."

Chapter Thirty-Five

When I arrived back in Charlotte, I was met by everyone with profound relief. My status as the chosen one by Jared seemed to be universally known at The Endless Night and I was suddenly treated differently. Melina later explained to me that, as a chosen companion, I would inherit everything including The Endless Night if anything ever happened to Jared. The idea of inheriting something like that terrified me.

Jared and I had a huge fight over whether I could stay on my own. I won it but with the compromise that I have my own security team. Peter got signed up for permanent guard duty. He started wearing the expression of a martyr. It was going to be a lot of growing pains as I figured out my role. It wasn't public, but there were whispers about Jared & me. Some good, some bad. The bad ones were more to do with me being a greedy gold digger.

The case with Natasha worked out better than anyone could have ever dreamed. She got to see her daughter. It turned out that the sack of shit she was married to arranged for the attack on Natasha except she was supposed to die. He had another girl that he was seeing secretly. Not only did she get to see her daughter, a plan to integrate Natasha with her daughter so she could have full custody was put into place. To make it even sweeter, Jared made sure she had a raise so that she had the income to support her daughter. Her ex-husband foamed at the mouth, cursed, and in general made an ass out of himself. Then he was arrested and charged. He is up on attempted murder charges among other things.

Spring was in the air and despite everything I managed to find time to do some reading for pleasure. I finally was going to read Pride & Prejudice. I often wondered what Granny would think of Jared. Would she approve or would she frown and tell me I should have known better? I rather think she would like him, though. "It is a truth universally acknowledged, that a single man in possession of a good fortune, must be in want of a wife."

The End

Authors Note:

Wow. It's been three years since I published the first book and I want to say it's been such a journey over those years. I really hope you enjoyed the book. I cannot express enough gratitude for those who have bought the books.

The next book is not going to be Jared and Cassandra. Instead it's going to be a Renaldo book. He's been telling me over and over for the last few years he isn't all bad and to give him a chance. So Renaldo and one other who shall not be named…. yet…will be stepping onto the stage. I do not have an ETA yet on when it will be published.

Thank you to my friends and family who have been supportive. My life would be very dark without you guys in it. Now onto the story of how a very socially awkward detective is caught. I wrote this story because a friend of mine complained that women never wanted the good guy. They only wanted to the bad boy. However, that's not always the case.

Anderson's Tale

By

Duchess MacKinnon

Chapter One

Detective Michael Anderson had a passion for law enforcement. He grew up reading Sherlock Holmes and could not remember a time when he wasn't going to be a cop. He was 25 when he achieved his dream. He entered the force with a master in criminal psychology. He quickly rose through the ranks but with some controversy. He knew from the start that his coping methods would cause a huge stir.

He had no idea how much of one. He was at a crime scene where a little girl was brutally murdered. He was certain that the live-in boyfriend was the one who did it. He wasn't even thinking about it when he did it. He was trying in fact to think of anything but how the poor little girl was brutally robbed. So, he wasn't even aware when he began to whistle, "Jingle Bells" at the crime scene. It wasn't until the mother was screaming in hysterics that he noticed. He was too distracted by the obvious signs of abuse of the child and how uncomfortable the live-in boyfriend was.

Unfortunately, it was a slow news week and the press who knew him just happened to be present. He was investigated because it became a major news story. Just to prove how slow of a news week it was, it even was talked about on the national stag. There wasn't anything he did that was legally wrong so there wasn't too much they could do. He could fight it under freedom of expression. It helped that he was right about the live-in boyfriend being the murderer. Corrective action went out the window when he was right a second time about the mother. The mother was part of the abuse.

It ultimately boiled down to his closure rate being one of the highest in the country. He wasn't interested in joining the FBI because his love for Charlotte was equal to his love of law enforcement. It also helped that his superiors didn't want to lose someone with that kind of statistic to another city. So, they proposed that he lead his own crime division.

It turned out that all the things that went bump in the night were real. Vampires were not just characters in fiction and as a result preternatural crime was a new field for law enforcement. They had problems with the preternatural squad and keeping a lead detective on it because they were completely untrained for this type of thing. It was viewed as the worst thing to happen to a detective. He wasn't happy with the promotion either but agreed if they would give him a preternatural consultant.

He suggested they try to lure Cassandra James away from Chicago. She was rumored to the best. It was not a popular initial suggestion because it was an underfunded division, however, a year later she interviewed for the job. It helped that their first consultant was a tremendous disaster and had caused the department additional embarrassment. He wasn't sure how much he could trust her but he was willing to give it his all. None of it was popular because in some quarters they viewed him a rogue cop being rewarded for bad behavior.

Surprising even to him, he liked the department. He realized quickly that he was bored to death with human crimes. They were too easy. A wife is murdered it was probably the husband. A child goes missing look close to home. It was too predictable.

The first time he encountered Melina was the first time he formally encountered Jared MacAllistair, the vampire king of Charlotte. It was a formal meeting because there was an ongoing investigation. When she walked into the room the first line he thought of was the urge to ask if it hurt when she fell from heaven because surely only angels were this beautiful. Yes, even he realized how lame that would sound and kept his mouth shut.

While she was of average height, there was a daintiness about her structure. She had light blonde hair that had a touch of honey and her eyes were a blue that reminded him of the ocean. He could drown in eyes like hers. It helped that she also had curves in all the right places. He forgot all about why he was there initially when Melina walked in like an angel. An angel that was on the arm of the vampire king.

He knew he wasn't ugly but he was by no means a competitor to Jared. There weren't too many men in the world who were. Detective Anderson was 5 feet 9 and while he tried to be fit he had to admit that he indulged just a little too much because he had a small spare tire though it now felt like a monster truck tire in the presence of someone as beautiful as Melina. Even her name was beautiful.

He only wished he had the opportunity to neaten up a bit and perhaps attempt to comb his unruly black hair. The only thing that didn't make him cringe was that he at least knew he had nice brown eyes. If she could get past his glasses that is. He made a mental note that perhaps he should try contacts again.

Chapter Two

Melina Fieriozza never had an easy life. She had no idea who her father was and her mother had drug problems. She was thrust in and out of foster homes for most of her life, some of them not better than what the state of California was rescuing her from. She was fifteen when she grew tired of it and decided to run away from the endless cycle of a new home and school every three to six months.

It was not one of her smartest decisions because it instantly made her vulnerable to predators. The first one she met was within the first day. His name was Marco and he was a were-leopard. At first she thought she loved him. But he didn't love her. He turned her into a shape-shifter within six months. Her life was a living hell for the next three years. He couldn't addict her to drugs because her metabolism burned through them but he did other things. He made her work as a prostitute and because of what she was she wouldn't get diseases. The healing abilities of shape-shifters was legend which on one hand was cool but on the other hand was unfortunate because he farmed her out to men who liked to abuse her.

Also, while healing abilities were great the fact is that a shape-shifter was only able to heal so much damage. Marco liked to push it to the edge. So much so that two of his girls had died in a six-month period and Melina knew that if she couldn't figure out how to get away she would sooner or later be killed. It was a close thing with her last client. It took her a week to heal. Marco was furious with her.

Then one day she felt him. He was in the city for a business. Marco felt him too and if she wasn't scheduled for a client she would be under lock and key like the others. It also helped that of all the girls she was the one who conformed the best. She never pushed the boundaries though it made Marco rather nervous. He liked the ones who were rebellious because he knew they were the ones who had to be watched the closest. He felt that Melina was just a little too compliant and that scared him. She was on a strict time line and was promised that if deviated she would pay dearly.

She dreaded going to this particular client and he was unfortunately one who requested her on a regular basis. He was the worst and sooner than later he was going to kill her. She had her options. She could make a break and run for it and pray she could get to the vampire king of Charlotte before she was taken.

She had no idea what she would do. Even as she dressed and was on her way to the client she didn't know. It wasn't until an unexpected opportunity happened. Jared was speaking three streets over from where her client was. The traffic was severely backed up. A matter that could be easily verified. So, she called Marco. "Marco I am in trouble. The traffic is so backed up I'm stuck. Can you tell Mr. Williams that I am on my way but just a little delayed? May I park the car and walk it so that I am not too late?"

It was a win / win situation for Melina. If Marco said yes she would walk as close as she could to the vampire king before removing her movement monitor. Then she would run for it. If he said no she would remove the monitor and leave. She knew she would have to leave everything behind. She only had to be brave and hope that Jared would take her.

"No Melina. I will call the client and let him know that you are delayed and why. You will stay put. I should have thought about the traffic and barricades."

Melina smiled. Marco fitted all his girls with a tracking bracelet. The only problem was that Melina learned how to slip hers off and she was careful enough that Marco never knew. She took a deep breath as her heart pounded. She had nothing left to lose. So, she ran. She ran through the streets until she approached the hotel that the conference was being held at. It wasn't as bad as she thought and she could feel him there. She concentrated with all her might to find Jared and she prayed he would pick up that she was looking for him. She was concentrating so hard she almost ran into Joe, one of the handlers that Marco employed.

Marco liked to employ men who weren't shafeshifters. They weren't a threat to his power and they were neutral when it came to anyone who could take them away from him. Of course, she should have known he would have precautions. It took Joe a second after she ran past him and into the hotel to realize who he had just seen before taking off after her. She could feel him chasing after her. She had one shot to find the vampire king.

She was running on near instinct when she burst into the conference room. Another being could not have looked more beautiful as Jared did in that instance. He represented the hope of being safe. Melina fell to her knees before him and said, "Master I am yours. Please accept me."

Melina was aware of Joe bursting into the conference room. "Forgive me sirs. My sister is a bit crazy in the head. She forgot to take her medicine." Melina prayed that the vampire king would not just accept his word.

"Somehow I don't think he is your brother or that you are crazy. What happens to you if I don't accept you?"

"I will die and it will not be fast. Please let me have a knife so that I can end my own life if you will not accept me. If they get me I will die slowly."

"That won't be necessary. I have this meeting to conclude but you will be cared for by Paul. Naomi is here as well. She is the alpha for my group."

Melina was escorted by two of Jared's team. She saw Joe glaring at her with animosity. It was several hours before she saw her new master and he was everything she had ever heard. She would die for him if need be and she would love him for saving her.

She told him about how she was made, what Marco did, and he promised that she would be safe. She was on an airplane when Jared told her that Marco was dead. He decided to shoot himself in the head it seems. Naomi read between the lines that Jared told him to do it and because leopards were his animal Marco had no choice but to comply.

She was given over to the care of Mary Anne who was Jared's personal assistant. It took time but Mary Anne was nearing retirement and Melina was chosen to be the one trained to be his personal assistant. It was an honor that gave her a purpose in life.

Chapter Three

The second-time Mike saw Melina was at dinner in Jared's private home. She sat next to him and chatted with him most of the night. She was smart, had a sense of humor, and was very likeable. When Mike received a call after dinner from Melina he thought something bad had happened. He winced when he thought of how he answered the phone. It had after all been just an hour departing from Jared's. "What's happened?"

"Happened?" A confused voice replied. To his credit he did figure out the cue that obviously, something didn't add up.

"Isn't that why you called?"

"Oh…you think something happened and I was notifying you."

"Isn't that why you are calling."

"No. I was hoping…. willyougooutwithmetomorrow?"

"Huh? I didn't quite catch that last part?" He did catch it but he was sure he needed to address an earwax problem since it sounded like she asked if he would go out with her tomorrow.

He heard Melina take a deep breath and she repeated, "Will you go out with me tomorrow? You can say no. I'll understand."

It wasn't often that Detective Mike Anderson was surprised in his life. He had to sit down for this one. All at once he went hot then cold. Then those pesky butterflies started. He hadn't felt this strange since he asked his first girl out.

He wasn't sure why she was asking him in the first place. He reviewed the evening. They talked and she paid a lot of attention to him but he didn't think he has said anything extraordinary. He thought she was being polite.

"Hello? Are you still there?" Melina asked.

"Yes I am here and yes tomorrow would be great. What time do you want me to pick you up?"

"Would seven work for you?"

"That works perfect for me. Err…do you have anything specific you would like to do?"

Melina thought kissing would be nice. What she said was, "Somewhere quiet so we can talk?"

"There is a really nice bistro that I go to occasionally. How about we go there and play the rest of it by ear?"

"That sounds great, Mike. I can't wait."

When Mike hung up the phone he could truly say was one of the craziest surreal things that could ever have happened to him. He even pinched himself to make sure he wasn't dreaming.

Chapter Four

Melina knew within minutes of when Cassandra James was shot. She knew because she felt the ripple of rage that Jared unleashed. It was unlike anything they had felt. They all had figured out that Jared very quickly had developed an interest in Cassandra. None had any idea how deep the interest was until that moment.

So, she was more than prepared when Anderson called to cancel on her. She was his partner even if she was just a consultant. He would be duty bound to be there personally for her. So, when Jared said to fix his schedule so he could go to the hospital, she flat out told him he was taking her with him. Which led to him examining her.

"Do you care to clue me in on the reason?"

Melina blushed and she couldn't refuse the question. "Yes. Detective Anderson has my attention."

"Really?!?" Melina couldn't help but flush because Jared had a very impressive tone of surprise.

"Yes really and why not? He has character and given his position integrity."

"I'm just teasing you Melina. Of course, you can come along and to give you the excuse to be there. Just promise me something. Let me know how shocked he is when you show up."

"Done."

And that was the start. She raided Bianca's kitchen for goodies to take with her. In one day, she became not just an angel but a savior from hospital cafeteria for Mike. When she showed up with non-hospital faire she knew she had won the first of many brownie points.

As they talked they found common interests and a mutual appreciation. Melina was glad that her original assessment of him was accurate. Jared approved and that made her comfortable because she trusted his opinion. For Mike, it was a relief that she was down to earth. She was still an angel but she was touchable.

They talked about almost everything but Melina felt some reluctance on Mike's part so she finally asked.

"Mike, why don't you kiss me?" She held her breath waiting. She wanted badly for him to kiss her.

Chapter Five

"Won't you get into trouble?" Detective Anderson asked with as much authority as he could. Melina exhaled slowly.

"Trouble? Why ever would you ask me that?"

Detective Anderson swallowed though he didn't know why. His mouth was bone dry from nervousness. "Aren't you and the vampire king an item?"

"An item? Do you mean his mistress?" Melina's mouth twitched from suppressed amusement. She knew he had some issues about her. She had no idea it was based on something as ludicrous as being Jared's mistress. She almost laughed out loud as Mike's hears turned red.

"Aren't you?"

Melina sighed since she knew he was serious and she was going to have to set some things straight. "Don't be silly. I work for him. He is my boss and what I do just requires me to be closer to him. Besides if you haven't noticed, he is dead gone over Cassandra James. Speaking of mistresses, how can I be sure she isn't your mistress?"

Mike was so shocked at being questioned about Cassandra he wasn't sure what to say. He adored his new partner and consultant. He couldn't have been more pleased. He even recognized that she was very attractive as well but he didn't think of her in that light. "Melina, I'm an officer of the law. I don't get paid well enough to keep a mistress. What on earth gave you the idea?"

"Hmmm…let's see. You are hanging around her bedside. She is not the least bit aware of Jared. "

"Oh she is aware of him alright," Anderson muttered.

"Does it bother you that she is?"

"Of course not. In fact, I think she might need him."

"She might be too screwed up. I know I was for a long time."

"You don't know the half of it," Anderson muttered as he thought of the scars he saw. Nobody survived something like that without being completely screwed up in some way.

"Mike, my job does require more contact with Jared than makes some comfortable" Melina swallowed hard and her heart was in her throat. "If this is a problem let me know now."

"It's not a problem. I only thought…" he saw her expression darken. "What I mean is…Jesus I am going to screw this all up. You are the most beautiful woman I've ever known I don't understand why Jared isn't with you or even that there isn't a long line. One so long that a mere detective would be truly desperate pickings."

Melina smiled. He was perfect for her. He might seem a little off but he wasn't. He was a solid man with a good heart. Yet he routinely saw the worst that mankind could dish out. He could handle her past and the world she was from.

"So it's settled then Mike? I'm going to be your girlfriend from now on?"

Mike knew the answer to that one and it was a resounding yes. "It's settled."

She was standing there with her head titled upward just a bit. Finally, she looked downward. "Mike? Aren't you going to kiss me?"

"Oh…. yes, I suppose I should if you want me too."

Mike intended to only give her a peck. It was the respectful thing to do. Melina knew him and that he didn't want to seem to be taking advantage.

"Mike do me a favor?"

"Anything."

"Make the kiss count."

Sometimes it might seem that the nice guy finishes last. That the bad boy is the one who always gets the girls. Sometimes though the nerdy geek who is a nice guy does finish first. Oh, and Detective Anderson did in fact make the kiss count.

www.ingramcontent.com/pod-product-compliance
Lightning Source LLC
Chambersburg PA
CBHW060824120626
46557CB00001B/353